UNMASKING LADY CAROLINE

Belles of Christmas Series

MINDY BURBIDGE STRUNK

Publisher's Note:

This is a work of fiction. Names, places and incidents are a product of the authors imagination. Locals and public names are sometimes used for atmospheric purposes, but any similarities to people-living or dead, business, events or locals are unintentional.

INTRODUCTION

This book is the first book in a series of five. All the books are stand
alone romances and can be read in any order. Make sure you read
them all:

Unmasking Lady Caroline
Goodwill for the Gentleman
The Earl's Mistletoe Match
Nine Ladies Dancing
A Duke for Lady Eve

ACKNOWLEDGMENTS

To Jenny Proctor, my fabulous editor who helps me with my comma addiction and love of em-dashes. She gives great insight when I need it most.

For my great writers' group: Dickens, Heyer, Bronte and Austen! You guys are my go to peeps. You keep me up in a business that easily gets you down and you're always there to make me laugh. You are truly my best friends!

To my proof-reader, Patti Knowlton. My grammar isn't getting any better, so I am very grateful yours is.

To my great ARC team. Thank you for all you do to help me be successful! I couldn't do it without you guys.

And last and most importantly, for my boys—big and little. Thanks for not complaining when you have to dig clean clothes out of the basket or get Raman for dinner...again. For reading over my shoulder and telling me you thought my story sounded 'really good.' For creating stories with me and giving my brain a break. And for encouraging me—telling me I 'made a good job choice to become an author.' I love you, tons! Especially to Christopher for supporting and helping me push through when it just fills too hard. For giving me the tools I need to make me successful. You are my greatest cheerleader! I couldn't do this without your support! LY

𝕾 I 𝕽

Lady Caroline Trowbridge lifted a hand, checking the fit of her mask as she watched her cousin dance with Mr. Benton. She let out a slight huff as she looked farther down the wall at the other chaperones and matrons, many of whom were not masked.

Why Prudence had insisted Caroline dress in costume was quite beyond her. Could she not have just come in her normal attire? Was the charade really necessary?

It was not as if she were some doe-eyed debutante in her first Season. She would not be sought after by the gentlemen here. At three and twenty, her parents, if not all of society, had her decidedly on the shelf—a condition which entailed lending her out as a companion to all and sundry. On this occasion, her cousin, Prudence.

Not for the first time, Caroline wished for a book or even a sampler to help occupy her time. It was not as if Mr. Benton would dare compromise Prudence in the middle of the dance floor.

A quiet snort pushed through Caroline's lips. *Prudence.* If ever there was a misnamed young lady, it was her cousin. Even now she was allowing Mr. Benton to finger the curl laying at the side of her cheek.

Caroline sighed and stood, just as Prudence caught her eye. The girl gave Mr. Benton a half-hearted push, raising a brow as she stared pointedly at Caroline.

Settling herself in her seat, Caroline shook her head, feeling the long peacock feathers on her mask sway back and forth. It was actions such as these that made her presence here necessary. She narrowed her gaze at the supposed gentleman, relaxing against the seat back when Mr. Benton led Prudence back to Caroline. The evening was sure to be an eternal affair.

Caroline took a long, deep, breath through her mouth, breathing it out through her nose. On the morrow they would depart for Long Compton to spend Christmas and Twelfth Night with her family. Even her brother, Samuel, and his wife would be in attendance.

"Cousin Caroline?" The sound of Prudence's voice brought another sigh to Caroline's lips.

Mr. Benton bowed. "Lady Caroline. I have returned your charge to your side, as promised." He turned back to Prudence and bowed over her hand, a look passing between them. "Miss Winslow." His voice sounded like honey—sweet and thick. He turned and moved toward the refreshment table.

Prudence dropped into the chair next to Caroline. "Must you be so proper all of the time? It was not as if Mr. Benton was doing anything so untoward."

"He was being precisely so." Caroline motioned toward the rest of the ballroom. "Do you see any other gentleman caressing the hair of young ladies?"

Prudence frowned.

"As I thought. I do not understand why you do not have enough sense to see it yourself."

Prudence gasped but Caroline had ceased caring about her directness weeks ago. She had come to London in early November with her uncle, at the opening of the current session of Parliament. In the beginning weeks, she had coddled Prudence, using gentler words when trying to correct her cousin's wilder ways. It had been for naught. The girl seemed determined to ruin herself and the whole of the family with her. It was something her uncle's political career could ill afford, and Caroline refused to sit by and allow it to happen.

"I cannot believe you would speak to me in such a manner." Prudence's lips pushed out in a pout.

"If you would use better judgment, I should not have to speak to you in such a way. I should think if someone had before now, perhaps you would have more sense in your brain box." Caroline looked around the ballroom, feeling no guilt for her reproof.

"I shall tell Papa of your cruelness as soon as we return home tonight. He will see you do not return with us after Twelfth Night."

Caroline hemmed. "If only I could be so fortunate, Cousin Prudence. But I fear you are mistaken."

Prudence turned away from Caroline, her arms folded over her chest. The girl knew Caroline was correct, even if they both wished it was not so.

Caroline forced herself to ignore the heavy sighs sounding beside her, instead watching the dancers. The ball was not as crowded as she would have suspected. Many of the ton must have decided to get an early start on their travels back to the country.

Her eyes traveled from one end of the ballroom to the other, then moved back to where they had started. Miss Emma Caldwell stood across the room, her face covered with a tiger mask. Her sister Lucy stood beside her. Why could Prudence not behave as the Caldwell girls?

Caroline's gaze continued around the room. Gentlemen dressed as wolves and foxes littered the edges of the dance floor. Even a large bear was in attendance.

Her gaze snapped back. There was something familiar about the furry creature. He was at least a head taller than anyone surrounding him, but when he sauntered around the outskirts of the room, Caroline's heart leapt into her throat. *It could not be him.*

She sucked in a breath.

A fur mask covered most of his face, but it was no matter; she would recognize that gait, those shoulders, anywhere. She had been watching them since she was barely out of leading strings.

Lord Creighton.

She bit the inside of her cheek. No, that was before his father's death. It was Lord Rockwell now. "Peter," she breathed out on a fluttering sigh.

Caroline fisted her hands, rubbing her damp palms with her fingers, small dots of moisture showing through her iridescent green-blue gloves. The gossips had said he was back, but she had yet to see him. In point of fact, she had not seen him in more than nine years. Not since he'd left for his tour of the continent.

"Cousin?" Prudence abandoned her own self-pitying long enough to impose herself on Caroline. "What has you so preoccupied? I am certain you have not heard a word I have spoken."

Caroline cleared her throat and smiled. "It is nothing. I only just remembered I forgot to purchase a present for Lydia."

Prudence waved her hand in the air. "There is still plenty of time for that, although you will not be able to purchase something from London. But there will be many shops on our way back."

Caroline nodded, but continued to watch the progression of

Lord Rockwell as he made his way around the room, stopping and chatting with groups as he went. If he continued on his current path, he would come upon her shortly.

A throat cleared and Caroline raised her gaze to Mr. Thurston. When had he come along?

"I understand Miss Winslow is hiding behind the panther mask." His head inclined toward Prudence. "Might I have the honor of the next set, Miss Winslow?"

Prudence looked pleadingly at Caroline. Caroline glanced back at the man with his high hairline and overly large nose. Mr. Thurston, it seemed, had not earned Prudence's affections.

A wicked sort of plan settled in Caroline's mind and she smiled up at Mr. Thurston. "Of course, Mr. Thurston. She would be delighted. Would you not, Cousin?"

She felt Prudence's displeasure beside her. Caroline placed her hand to her lips, hiding a wide smile. She elbowed her cousin in the ribs. "Are you not delighted, Miss Winslow, to have been singled out by Mr. Thurston?"

Prudence spoke through gritted teeth. "Yes, thank you for the honor, Mr. Thurston."

He extended a hand and led Prudence to the dance floor. She glared at Caroline from over her shoulder.

Caroline laughed, relieved that she need not pay as close attention to her cousin for at least this set. Mr. Thurston was a gentleman and a complete bore; he would do nothing questionable to Prudence.

"Please, do share your joke with me."

Caroline jerked her head to the side even as the deep, rich voice flooded her brain. How had Peter sidled up beside her without her knowing? Curse her need to teach Prudence a lesson. "I do not believe you will find it so very witty, my lord. It was a personal joke between my cousin and me."

MINDY BURBIDGE STRUNK

"Perhaps I can be the judge of that." His voice was like warm, smooth custard.

Caroline nearly melted into her seat. Gooseflesh broke out on her arms and legs. That voice—it felt so fresh in her mind it was as if she had heard it only yesterday, rather than nearly a decade ago. She offered a stuttering laugh. "I was only chuckling because my cousin did not wish to dance with Mr. Thurston, but I accepted on her behalf, anyhow. She was not pleased with me when she left on his arm." Caroline smiled again at the memory.

Lord Rockwell grinned. "Ah, you see, I am able to find the humor in it."

She shook her finger at him. "A mere smile does not indicate humor, my lord. Had you truly thought it funny, I should think you would laugh."

"Perhaps had I seen your cousin's face, I should have laughed also." He tilted his head to the side, a half-smile on his face. The small indent formed beside his lip—that same one he'd had since childhood. Caroline refrained from touching it.

"Would you do me the honor of dancing the next set with me?"

Dance with Peter? She could never refuse him such a request. In truth, there was very little she would deny him. Caroline opened her mouth to respond but he continued.

"I know we have not, as yet, been properly introduced. But given the masks, will anyone be the wiser?"

She snapped her mouth shut and frowned. What did he mean they had not been properly introduced? "Surely, you are in jest, my lord."

He eyed her. "How do you know I am a lord if we have not yet met?" His dark green eyes flickered with questions.

"Perhaps because I know who you are, Lord Rockwell. Your mask does not have me fooled."

His mouth dropped open slightly and she reached up and pinched it shut with her thumb and forefinger. The feel of his skin, with a hint of stubble poking at her finger, sent a jolt up her arm.

"You find me at a disadvantage, Miss. For you know my name, but I do not know yours."

Caroline squinted at him. Was he merely teasing her? He stared at her intently, recognition noticeably absent from his gaze. "Truly, you do not know? How can this be so?"

"It seems we have been introduced. But when? I am afraid your mask conceals your identity too well." He tried to look around it, but the mask was fitted too closely to her face. "Please, be so kind as to tell me your name."

A playful thought entered Caroline's mind, although her mother would surely call it wicked. When had she become such a lady? She was not usually one to play such games. But she could not help herself. She grinned and shook her head. Perhaps this evening could be entertaining after all. "If you cannot remember, I shall not be the one to tell you. Perhaps, after we dance, you will be able to deduce it."

He huffed out a shallow breath. Peter never had been one to wait. "If you will not tell me, what am I to call you?"

Caroline put a finger to her mouth. Her stomach gave a lurch when she saw his eyes follow. "You may call me Miss... Tree." A giggle gurgled in her throat, but someone of her maturity did not giggle, so she pushed it down. Instead, she arched a brow at him.

He rubbed at his chin where she had touched him earlier, then held out his arm to her. "Very well, Miss Tree—" he chuckled and paused. "You are a clever one."

"Not to worry." Caroline laughed. "I am sure you will figure it out soon enough, Lord Rockwell."

They took their place in line, waiting only a moment for the music to begin. Every time they came together, he asked her a question. "Where are you from, Miss Tree?"

"The country."

They separated and Caroline came together with the dour Lord Figgins. A small frown perpetually pulled down his lips.

When she met Lord Rockwell again, he wasted no time. "What are you doing in London, Miss Tree?"

"I am come with my uncle and cousin for the Parliamentary session. My cousin is in great need of a chaperone." He nodded his head in thought as they separated once again.

They came back together and touched palms. "Is your uncle in Lords?"

Caroline shook her head. "He is serving in Commons." She almost felt guilty when his face fell. He must have figured he had a chance of discovering her, if her uncle were a Lord. But he seemed less confident with Commons.

As they separated again, his brow furrowed. Caroline swallowed hard. How many times had she seen that exact look on his face? She did not know how long she could hold him off, but she intended to enjoy it while she could.

Mr. Hardy now stood in front of her. He smiled at her and she returned it half-heartedly. Her eyes darted down the line, watching Peter as he smiled at another masked lady. Was he intrigued by the young lady? He seemed to smile at her in the same manner as he had Caroline. The thought made her look away, but she glanced back again. He did not speak to the lady. That must imply something, certainly.

They came back together. "Are you to stay in London for the holiday, Miss Tree?"

Caroline shook her head, a small smile on her face. "No. I am to return to the country first thing on the morrow."

"Which county will you be returning to?"

Caroline bit her lower lip. Did she dare tell him the county? Would it be enough to give her away? "I will be going north, my lord."

He gave a frustrated grunt as they touched palms and walked around in a circle. "How far north?"

"Not as far as Scotland, but farther north than Oxfordshire."

"You are most vexing, Miss Tree." His face hinted at amusement, but she could see his irritation mounting. It seemed Peter was still not used to waiting for things. "Will you be returning to London after Twelfth Night?" His eyes were hopeful, and Caroline's face fell. Would he look so hopeful if, rather, *when*—for surely it was only a matter of time —he discovered it was her beneath the mask?

"Not if my cousin has any say in the matter." She pushed her doubts away and grinned. "I am sure after the trickery with Mr. Thurston, she will be demanding I stay behind."

"Surely it is not as bad as all that."

They separated again, giving Caroline a moment to steady her breathing and her pulse. It hardly seemed real that Peter was dancing with her now. She smiled politely at the gentleman in front of her. Their group of four formed a small circle, each putting a hand into the middle. Her hand rested atop Peter's and a swarm of butterflies fluttered in her stomach. They walked in a circle and Caroline could feel Peter's eyes on her. She kept her gaze directed at a small woven flower on the Persian rug, afraid he would know her thoughts if she caught his eye.

They all turned and changed the direction of their walk, forcing Caroline to withdraw her hand from Peter's. Disappointment pushed the butterflies down when her hand became sandwiched between Lord Figgins's and Miss Langston's. She chanced a glance at Peter, stumbling for several steps when he caught her looking at him.

After what felt like an eternity, Caroline came face to face with Peter again. He grinned down at her. "Perhaps if you tell me your uncle's name, I could convince him to bring you back to London after the holiday."

Caroline smiled. What had she been thinking when she began this charade? Eventually he would discover her identity and then what would he think? He would, no doubt, lose all interest. Had he not told her years ago there could be nothing more between them than friendship? "You are shrewd, my lord. But I will not fall for your trickery."

His shoulders sagged exaggeratedly. "But how am I to discover who you are?"

Caroline bit her lower lip. "If you have not discovered it before the end of the night, I shall make myself known once we return to London from the country."

He frowned. "But that is more than a fortnight. How am I to wait so long?"

Caroline walked around him in a circle, stopping when she stood in front of him again. She tsked. "I see you are still impatient, my lord. I should have thought you would have outgrown that trait as you got older."

His frown deepened. "How do you know such things?" Again, he tried to peer around her mask.

Caroline turned her head with him, her eyes catching sight of Prudence just as she slipped from the ballroom. Mr. Benton followed close behind. Gah! The foolish girl.

Caroline dropped her hand and took several steps back. "I'm sorry, my lord, but I must go. My cousin has just made a most impudent decision. Please, forgive my rudeness." She dashed away from the line of ladies, leaving Peter standing without a partner, staring after her.

❧ 2 ❧

Peter handed off his horse to the groomsman standing just inside the stables. He pulled his greatcoat tighter around him, unable to keep the chill at bay as he had done while riding from London. He had even allowed himself time to think on the mysterious young woman from Lord Trenton's ball. It was not hard to stay warm when thoughts of her swirled around in his mind. Had she given him her name or if she had been staying in London for the holiday, he might have canceled this trip back to Wirksworth Hall in order to discover her identity and perhaps even court her.

He shook his head in frustration. It had been a long time since he had found someone so intriguing, someone he was actually interested in advancing an acquaintance. But the impossible lady had not even given him her name. Why? What did she have to gain by her little game?

While he was beyond frustrated by it, his interest in her pushed those frustrations aside. For now.

He had considered searching for her in the country, but he

knew not which county she resided in and there were many counties between Oxfordshire and Scotland. The task was daunting, even for the likes of Peter.

The wind blew through his coats as if they were made of the thinnest fabrics, and not the finest woolens available in England. He could not continue to stand about wool-gathering in this weather.

He jogged across the yard and walked up the steps of Wirksworth, stopping halfway up. He leaned heavily against the thick stone railing, looking up at his childhood home. How had he been away for nearly ten years? Memories of running down the stairs after Montjoy or little Lady Caroline, on their way to an adventure of their own making brought a smile to his lips. But it was short lived as a heaviness pressed down on his shoulders. Not all his memories were pleasant ones.

The house looked just as it always had, even though his father had been dead for nearly seven months—not that he had lived here much since he remarried. His father, or rather, his stepmother had preferred the house in Kent, to the family seat here in Warwickshire.

Peter ran his fingers over the smooth stonework and sucked in a deep breath, pushing himself to continue the rest of the way up the stairs. At least he need not worry about seeing his stepmother inside. The thought of spending the holidays in *her* presence nearly made him turn back toward the stables and his horse.

After one firm rap of the knocker, Porter, the butler, pulled the door open. His stoic face relaxed into a smile—or as much of a smile as Porter ever allowed to grace his face. The man was nothing, if not proper.

"My lord, it is good to have you home again." The door opened wider and Peter stepped inside, immediately soaking in the smell of furniture polish and lavender. He half-expected his mother to come gliding down the staircase at any moment. How, after all these years, did the house still smell of her?

"It is good to be home, Porter. I apologize for my early arrival. I had intended to spend a few more days in London, but when Parliament adjourned, I found I could not stomach the stale London air another day."

Mrs. Harris entered the grand entryway, a vase of lavender and white roses in her hands. That must be why the house smelled as it did.

"Lord Creighton? You are returned." She smiled and then corrected herself. "Begging your pardon, Lord Rockwell." A sentimental look entered her eyes. "Look at you, lad. You are a man now."

Peter chuckled and dropped a kiss on the housekeeper's cheek. A part of him wished he could wrap his arms around her and hold her tightly. But he didn't. Such an action would be immensely improper.

Instead he smiled down at her. "I was a man before I left, Mrs. Harris. Perhaps now I am just portlier." Peter patted his flat stomach.

"We can agree to disagree, my lord." She patted his cheek. Before her elevation to above-stairs maid and then housekeeper, Mrs. Harris had helped in the nursery. Peter had spent almost as much time in her care, as his mother's when he was young. "You are right, I suppose." Peter screwed up his mouth to one side. "In stature I may have been a man, but most certainly not in wisdom. I hope in that respect I have changed."

Porter cleared his throat, interrupting their pleasant reunion. "Mrs. Harris, is his lordship's chambers ready?"

The housekeeper scowled at the butler but turned back to Peter and nodded. "I took the liberty of moving your things into the master's room. I hope that is what you wished." A shadow of doubt washed over her face. "If not, I shall see everything returned to the way you left it in your previous room, my lord."

Peter shook his head. "All is well, Mrs. Harris." It would feel odd to reside in his father's old chambers, but Peter guessed it was what was to be expected. He was the earl, now, was he not? "Besides, I do not believe I even recall my room's appearance when last I left." His face colored up slightly at the memory of storming from the house all those years ago. At the time, he had not intended to stay away so long. Looking back, it had been a childish tantrum which took him away from Wirksworth. But what was done was done. He was back now and ready to assume the role he had been born to.

Mrs. Harris nodded and excused herself to check on the maids working in the guest wing.

Peter started up the stairs to his father's study—*his* study. Was this how he would think of everything?

He walked down the corridor. The house was completely still, but instead of feeling peaceful, it felt cold and lonely. Peter swallowed hard and turned on his heel. The ledgers could wait until evening. For now, he needed noise; he needed people about.

He made his way back toward the entryway, hollering for Porter as his foot settled on the travertine floor.

The butler emerged from a nearby room, his brow furrowed. The long absence of a master must have left the man's instinct a bit rusty.

"Porter, do you know if Lord Killingsworth and his family are at their estate for the holidays?"

The butler nodded. "Lord and Lady Killingsworth are at Whitley Wood. I understand Lord Montjoy and his wife will be arriving shortly, if they have not already."

Peter smiled. He had scarcely seen Montjoy in London. Because Montjoy held only a courtesy title, he was not seated in

Lords, and they had attended very few of the same parties. It would be wonderful to spend time with his oldest friend.

Perhaps the holidays would not be so lonely after all. "What of Lady Caroline? Is she in residence?"

The butler nodded. "Yes, my lord."

Peter grinned. Then things would be just as they always had been. A visit to Whitley Wood was in order. Even if Montjoy was not yet arrived, little Lady Caroline would surely prove better than no one. He grinned, remembering the little girl in braids who used to follow Montjoy and him around. Peter's brow creased. Little Lady Caroline. She must be close to coming out by now. He found the notion disturbing.

The thought of Caroline being *properized* made Peter scowl. He could not imagine the freckle-faced girl he knew curtsying and doing everything else required of a proper debutante.

Peter shrugged. "Fetch me my greatcoat and beaver, Porter. I believe I shall go and visit the marquess."

"Do you wish me to have the carriage readied, my lord?"

Peter shook his head. "It is barely five miles to Whitley Wood. And that is if I take the main road. I will take the back path and be there before the carriage could even be pulled from the carriage house."

He pulled on his wool lined gloves, interlocking his fingers as he pushed them farther inside. As he stepped out the door, a gust of wind nearly took his hat. Peter put his hand on top, while his other hand pulled his greatcoat tighter around him. The snow that crunched beneath his boots confirmed his suspicions. It was to be a cold winter this year.

The wind at his back made him step quicker, getting him to Whitley Wood much faster than was normal. As he approached the ancient castle, he looked up at its rounded walls. The circular design was less common in castle design, even on the continent.

His eyes drifted to the drawbridge tower. How many hours had they spent charging up and down those stairs as children?

The drawbridge was down, as was customary in the daylight hours. He crossed over into the courtyard, a sense of nostalgia overtaking him. Whitley Wood had not changed a whit in the last two hundred years, at least.

Taking the wooden stairs two at a time, he knocked firmly on the door. A footman in deep blue and silver livery opened the door only wide enough to see Peter, but not enough to allow the cold inside.

Peter did not recognize the man. The marquess must have hired new servants while Peter had been away. He shrugged, unsure why the notion surprised and even unsettled him. Ten years was a long time. Had he really thought nothing would change in his absence?

Peter stepped forward and handed over his card. The footman read it and nodded, opening the door wide enough to allow Peter entrance. "Please follow me, my lord."

The footman led him down a long corridor, no doubt to the Green Parlor. Peter smiled as he thought back on all the time he had spent running about these passageways with Montjoy and little Lady Caroline, Nurse Garvey hollering after them to come back and tugging on their ears once she'd caught them.

The footman motioned Peter into a small parlor to wait as he pushed through the doorway across the corridor. Instead, Peter stayed where he was, listening in as the footman announced Peter to Lord Killingsworth. The older man's boisterous voice could be heard through the crack in the door. "Of course. Show Lord Rockwell in, Harry."

"Yes, my lord."

Peter quickly stepped inside the parlor, pretending to have

been waiting patiently. It seemed this old castle brought out his less dignified manners, even still.

Harry stepped just inside the door and motioned to Peter with his head. "Right this way, my lord."

They walked across the corridor and Harry opened the door to the Green Parlor, motioning Peter forward.

Peter stepped inside, his gaze scanning the room. An instant warmth settled over him. This is what he needed. This is what was lacking from Wirksworth.

"Ah, Lord Rockwell. Welcome." Lord Killingsworth stood and walked toward Peter, clasping him on the back as he shook his hand. "It has been a long time." Killingsworth's smile dropped. "I am sorry about your father."

Peter shrugged, shaking off the dark mood the mention of his father brought on. "It is good to be home, my lord." He looked toward the settee by the fireplace, spotting Lady Killingsworth standing next to Lady Montjoy. Peter recognized her from the few times they had crossed paths in London.

He surveyed the room, looking for Lady Caroline. His eyes passed over a lovely lady reading a book in a chair on the opposite side, but he continued around the room. His eyes came back to the lady several times. She was quite exquisite, but Lady Caroline did not seem to be present. Perhaps she was out visiting or in the library. He remembered she had been fond of reading.

He walked toward the settee and bowed to Lady Killingsworth. "Lady Killingsworth. You have not changed a whit in all these years."

A smile turned up only the very tips of her lips, making Peter question if it was actually a smile at all. She rapped at his arm with her fan. "You are quite the charmer, my lord, just as your father was."

Peter's smile dropped and his body stiffened. Was that how he came across? As a philandering rake?

Lady Killingsworth motioned with her head to the lady next to her. Peter relaxed slightly. "Lord Rockwell, my daughter-in-law, Lady Montjoy."

Peter nodded. "Yes, we met briefly in London—at the Jones's card party, I believe."

Lady Montjoy nodded and smiled. "It is lovely to see you again, my lord."

Lady Killingsworth motioned to the lady across the room and Peter's pulse quickened for a few beats.

"I am sure you remember my daughter, Lady Caroline, do you not?"

Peter snapped back, as if he had been slapped. He squinted at the lady now standing only a rods length away. "Little Lady Caroline?" He swallowed. What had happened to the freckles? Only one remained, sitting daintily above her upper lip. Gone also were the plaits down each side of her head, replaced by a few curls which framed her face. What happened to the awkward little girl he remembered?

One brow rose and her lips twitched. "Lord Rockwell. How pleasant it is to see you after all these years."

"Y...yes. And...and you, Lady Caroline." He looked her over again. Beneath her gown, it was obvious she had curves—rather remarkable curves. His face heated all the way to the tips of his ears at the thought. He raised his gaze back up to hers. Something did not feel right about thinking of little Lady Caroline in such a way.

"Lord Rockwell, would you please stay for supper? We have much to catch up on." She grinned wickedly at him, almost as if she knew a secret he did not.

He swallowed hard and tucked a finger between his collar and his neck. This was not what he had envisioned when he set out from Wirksworth. "When did you say Montjoy would be arriving?"

Lady Caroline shifted on her feet, looking at him with the same deep blue eyes she had always had. It felt both comforting and disquieting. Things felt different now. He felt different somehow.

"Samuel is here. He is attending to some business in town. He will return before dinner if it makes a difference to you."

The face and the body may be older, more mature, but Peter could still see a hint of the mischievous little scamp of all those years ago.

"I should be honored to join you. I do not mind admitting that Wirksworth is a bit too quiet. I should be glad for the company."

A full, wide smile spread across Lady Caroline's face and Peter felt his pulse skitter again. He frowned. What was that all about? Perhaps he needed to seek the counsel of Doctor Hastings on the matter.

$\mathscr{H}$ 3 $\mathscr{H}$

C aroline could not help smiling as she spooned the soup into her mouth. The shock on Peter's face when he saw her earlier still brought her joy.

A throat cleared from across the table and Caroline raised her gaze. Peter looked at her. He smiled, but still his look held one of surprise—like one about to be run over by a carriage. It was as if he did not believe she could have grown while he was away.

Or perhaps he was simply surprised she had aged so much. Her smiled dropped. She lifted the glass of claret, discreetly checking her reflection. That notion seemed more logical than the idea that he liked what he saw. He would have to be daft to believe she had not aged while he was away.

Samuel, Peter and her father did most of the talking throughout supper. They spoke first of matters currently being addressed in Parliament and then moved on to the spring planting.

Caroline was content to sit and observe, sneaking peeks of Peter when he was not watching, making up for the nearly ten years in which she had been unable to do so.

She was quite disappointed when it came time for the ladies to retire to the drawing room while the men drank their port. But then, perhaps her eyes needed a change of scenery so they might be prepared to gaze on him again when the men joined them.

Harry pulled her chair out as she stood. She nodded to her father and brother, then turned her gaze to Peter.

He looked at her again, his brow furrowed, before his face relaxed into a small smile.

Caroline followed her mother and Lydia out of the room. When they entered the drawing room, each went in search of their separate interests. Lydia retrieved her sewing basket, as did Lady Killingsworth. Caroline retrieved her book from the window seat at the far side of the room. They all came together, each taking a seat on a different settee forming a U in front of the fireplace.

"Really, Caroline. It is no wonder you have not received an offer in over a year. You have nothing to offer a gentleman if your nose is always in a book." Her mother tsked and sighed as she placed her spectacles upon the end of her nose.

Caroline picked up her book. It was the same reprimand she'd received each night since returning from London. While she despised watching over Prudence, the task had at least allowed Caroline to remove herself from under her mother's critical eye. She knew her mother expected no reply, so she gave none. It was enough for her mother to just have her say.

Caroline looked at the words on the page but paid them little heed as she listened to her mother and sister-in-law's conversation.

"With Lord Killingsworth's numerous illnesses this past year, I think it prudent for you to begin your training, Lady Montjoy. I have advised Lord Killingsworth to do the same with Montjoy."

Caroline cautioned a glance at her sister-in-law, questioning her reception to the formalities her mother insisted upon.

Lydia continued her stitching, nodding her head in agreement.

She seemed quite at ease with all the lady this and lord that which Caroline's mother insisted upon.

"I think our most urgent matter will be that of the tenant's baskets. We will want to have them ready before Christmas, so we can deliver them on Boxing Day."

Caroline looked up at her mother and nodded her head. She opened her mouth to respond, but her face slackened when she realized it was Lydia who was the intended recipient of the remark.

"I am ready when you feel it necessary, my lady. But I do not want you to feel as though you are being driven from your home." Lydia, always the diplomat, let her stitchery fall into her lap. It was obvious from the light in her eyes, she had been anticipating this for some time. What woman did not anticipate the time she would become mistress?

Lady Killingsworth stopped her stitching as well and patted her daughter-in-law on the hand. "I should never feel anything of the sort, my dear." She sighed, her voice taking on a weepy tone. "I only pray I am wrong and Lord Killingsworth is still long for this world."

Caroline pushed down the snort forming in the back of her throat. While her parents got on well enough, theirs was not a love match. What her mother implied, but would never say aloud, was that she only prayed her husband would not die because she did not want to lose her place as mistress of Whitley Wood.

"We all pray for that, Lady Killingsworth." Lydia pulled her stitchery back up to her face, looking intently at it. But Caroline could see the smile curling up the corners of her sister-in-law's mouth.

Breathing slowly through her slightly parted lips, Caroline focused on the words in her book. But the scrutiny did not last long as her mind swirled. What was she to do with herself this holiday?

If mother was to train Lydia, they would not only be making the tenant's baskets, but also assume the tasks of trimming the house for the festivities and purchasing presents for the servants. It left little for Caroline to do.

She tried to push the hurt and loneliness away, but it settled on her shoulders anyhow. It only served to point out the obvious. She was to become a greater burden with every passing year. If only Caroline were comfortably situated—

She shrugged her shoulders, cutting off her own thoughts with a quiet huff. What was done was done. And even still, she did not believe she had been wrong in turning down the proposals.

The door opened and the men came into the room. Caroline's spirits lifted slightly. Although she continued to hold her book in front of her face, she watched them—or rather one of them—from the corner of her eye.

Her heartbeat picked up. She could feel it thumping in her neck and wrists as he came closer. She sucked in a long, slow breath through her teeth. Why was she acting in such a manner? It was not as if she had not been around handsome gentlemen before.

But this was *Peter*. She had not been around him in so long.

Focusing on her book again, she scolded herself quietly. She had long since abandoned her childish notions about him. She glanced in his direction and found him staring at her. Her cheeks flushed and she questioned the truthfulness of her previous thoughts.

Samuel took the seat next to his wife. A proper distance remained between them. Caroline often wondered after her brother. Why had he let their mother choose whom he would marry? Samuel was not the romantic type but still, Caroline had thought he would choose his own wife. She had hoped he would marry for love.

Samuel smiled at his wife and she returned it. At least they seemed to get along well. Perhaps, in time theirs would grow into a marriage of love. Caroline hoped it would be so.

The cushion on the settee depressed, shifting Caroline toward it.

She glanced over and her breath caught in her throat.

Peter sat next to her, one leg crossed over the other and his hands clasped together over his knee.

"Little Lady Caroline," he mused and then cleared his throat. "The name does not seem to fit so well anymore."

She dropped her book, but not all the way into her lap. It felt safer to have it at the ready, should she need it. "Lady Caroline is preferable." She raised a brow at him. "But then, it always was. You, however, did not seem to care that I detested being called 'little'. Indeed, I think it only added to the humor for you."

A lopsided smile formed on his lips. "I still believe you secretly liked it."

Caroline shrugged. Perhaps she had. Any attention she received from Peter had been more than welcome. But she would never confess such things to him. "How did you find Wirksworth Hall? Was this the first you have seen it since you have returned?"

He nodded his head slowly, as if thinking something through. "Yes. When I returned, I went straight for London. Parliament was convening and I had no time to return to Long Compton first." A wistful smile touched his lips. "But to answer your first question, Wirksworth is well—better than I had anticipated, in fact."

Caroline played with the corners of the pages of her book, now lying in her lap. She had apparently let her guard down already. She frowned. That had not taken very long. "You have employed a capable staff. I am certain things were just as they should have been."

"It still smells of lavender." His voice was quiet, as if he were speaking his thoughts inadvertently. He glanced at her and ran a hand through his hair. She had missed that gesture over the years. His slightly curly hair bounced back into place, save one rebellious tuft. "It is only one of the many things I find I miss about my mother, of late."

Caroline wanted to reach out and touch him, give his arm a squeeze, fix the unruly tuft of hair, anything to let him know she understood—or sympathized, perhaps, was a better word. She did not, in point of fact, understand the loss of a parent. She had not lost her mother nor her father. Not that she would understand Peter's sadness, even if she had. She did not share the same closeness with her mother which Peter had shared with his.

"I am sorry it was hard for you." Caroline bit her lower lip and stared at her book. She did not know what else to say.

He shrugged. "I did not intend to bring your mood down. It is not all gloom and doom. There are many happy memories at Wirksworth. I find I am very glad to be back."

Caroline glanced up at him. "I am surprised you were to come home for the holidays. I thought you to stay in town for the short recess." She returned her gaze to her abandoned barrier that sat in her lap. Why had she dropped it there? Now would be the perfect time for its usefulness. But the act would be far too obvious, should she try to use it. "What of your sister? Is she not to visit? I should think her anxious to see you after all these years."

Peter looked at the book in her lap and then to her face. Did he understand what she had been thinking? The slight grin seemed to indicate he just might.

"No, she seemed content to stay in London. If we had not seen each other while there then perhaps she would have come, but as it is, she did not want to make the journey. She thought it too difficult with the children."

They sat in silence for several moments. A heavy sigh sounded next to her and she glanced over at him, her brow raised in question.

"I am sorry. I was just thinking on all the things I must do. I had not realized all that coming home would entail when I first set out from London."

Caroline put her book on the side table next to her, abandoning the idea of using it for any sort of interference. "I thought you said Wirksworth had been well taken care of in your absence."

"It has. It is not the estate of which I speak." Peter shifted and turned on the cushion to face her. "It is the holiday and all that it entails. There are tenant's baskets to prepare, presents for the staff, the servants' ball and trimming the house for the holidays. That is nothing to planning the annual Twelfth Night ball at Wirksworth Hall." With each item he listed, his shoulders slumped a little more. "I understand the ball has not been held for several years." He frowned, running his thumb in circles over his knee. "It seems my father was unable to be bothered with it. The influence of his wife, no doubt."

The earlier desire to touch or comfort him, returned and Caroline leaned forward slightly. "I could help you with some of it..."

His eyes flew up to meet hers and she realized the untowardness of her offer. She shook her head. This was not how things had been before he left. The offer would not have felt improper all those years ago. It would simply have been a friend helping another friend. But now? She leaned back, putting distance between them. "I apologize. I am sure you have everything completely under control."

His eyes went wide and his head shook quickly. "No. I am the complete opposite of in control. I have no notion even where to begin or what to do." He scooted closer to her on the settee, a wild look in his eyes. "Please?" He glanced over at her mother and his form crumpled slightly. "It is I who should apologize now. I am sure you do not have time to spare for me. Your mother surely requires your help with those same tasks here at Whitley."

Caroline relaxed against the back cushion. Could he really be in need of her help? Did he desire it, or had he just sensed she was feeling alone? "No. My mother has enlisted Lydia to help with things here at Whitley Wood. I am not otherwise engaged."

The tension in his features relaxed and he nodded. "Then I should be very grateful to you." He leaned in slightly. "I know nothing of what I am to do. It is the tenants and servants who will be in your debt, if I am to be honest. They would be thoroughly disappointed were I to be left in charge."

The earlier weight on her shoulders lifted and she felt a lightness that had not been present in years. "What shall we do first?"

Peter shrugged, his eyes full of uncertainty. "I have no idea. I had hoped you would know."

Caroline laughed. "Very well, then I believe we should plan and purchase the supplies for the tenant's baskets and also shop for the servants' gifts."

Peter nodded. "That sounds like the best plan." He turned his gaze back on her. "Shall we go into the village on the morrow?"

Caroline nodded. "Yes. I fear if we wait much longer, the snow which is sure to come, will cause us trouble."

Peter rubbed his hands up and down his legs. "Yes. You are right. We should not delay any longer. Shall I fetch you after breakfast, then?"

Caroline felt the air leave her lungs at the thought of being alone with Peter in the carriage all the way to the village. But then she realized Barton would likely be sent along with them. It was less exciting, but still the air did not come easily to Caroline's chest. Perhaps it best to avoid Peter's carriage altogether. "I have a few presents still to purchase. Perhaps I could meet you in the village?"

Peter's smile dropped a fraction but returned quickly. Was he disappointed she would not be traveling with him? It was more likely she had reminded him of a present he had missed purchasing.

Caroline forced her pounding heart to calm down. There was nothing here, nothing for her to get excited about. She was only helping an old friend.

Peter stood and everyone stood with him. "It is getting late. I should be returning to Wirksworth." He stood and bowed to her, then her mother and Lydia. "Thank you for the invitation tonight."

He turned and left the room.

Samuel did not take up his seat next to his wife. Instead, he sat down next to Caroline. He leaned in close so his words would not be overheard. "I see the way you look at him."

Caroline feigned ignorance. "I have no notion of what you speak."

Samuel leveled his gaze. "Come now, Caroline. I know you thought yourself in love with him at one time. I only mean to warn you, lest you fall under his spell again."

Caroline turned away from her brother. "I am in no danger." She frowned. "But what do you have to warn me about? Peter was...*is* your best friend, is he not?"

Samuel nodded. "Yes, of course. But there are tales being bandied about the *Ton*—accusations that do not put him in a complimentary light."

"What stories, Samuel?" She shook her head. "I did not think you one to listen to the latest on-dit."

"It is not gossip. At least not all of it. There is a young lady he brought over from France. She is currently living with his sister. I've heard tale Lady Kirtley is sponsoring her for the season."

Caroline guffawed. "I do not see the point in any of this. What does that matter?"

"It is possible he has brought her here to court her." He sighed. "I only mean to protect you, Caroline. Just be careful where Peter is concerned."

Was it true? Had Peter sent for a French lady to marry? She swallowed, the tightness in her throat making it nearly impossible. Why was she disappointed? Did she not already know he would never be more than her friend? Why could she not seem to remember that one important thing?

4

Peter stepped down from the carriage, straightening his waist coat as his foot connected with the ground. He would have preferred to ride his horse into the village, but with the amount of purchases he intended to make, he thought it best to have the carriage.

He made a cursory glance around the main street. Was Miss Tree in a village similar to this? Was it possible she was in this village? He shook his head. Would he even recognize her if she were here? Her mask had covered most of her face, leaving very little for him to recognize her by. Perhaps her blue eyes would be enough? They had been very captivating.

Looking around the village, no one seemed likely to be Miss Tree, a most disappointing notion, indeed. He walked several rods down the walk.

The village of Long Compton had changed very little in the last ten years. He did not know what he had expected, but it was not that everything would be exactly as it had been before he left

England. He smiled at the comfort that came from knowing where every shop was and likely even knowing its proprietor.

He walked to the bakery, hoping to arrive before Caroline. As he approached the shop, he glanced through the window. A woman stood at the counter with her back to him. A bonnet and heavy woolen cloak covered any discernible features, until she turned her head slightly and he caught a glimpse of her profile. Caroline.

Peter stopped in his tracks, content to watch her from a distance for a moment. Perhaps it was fortuitous that he had not arrived first and been robbed of this moment. He'd had little chance to observe her discreetly the night before, as her family was always near for the whole of the evening. He reached up and straightened his cravat, bouncing his gaze back and forth between her and checking his reflection in the glass.

He was having a difficult time reconciling the gangly little girl, with the woman standing at the counter.

The years had been kind to her. In addition to the change in her figure, her hair had darkened ever so slightly. Perhaps it was because she did not spend as much time in the sunshine as she had when she was a girl. The freckles had disappeared, and her eyes had seemed to brighten with the passing of time.

She was not what he had planned on meeting when he came into Warwickshire. Indeed, after seeing her, he was surprised she was not married with a family of her own.

He shifted and she must have caught the movement from the corner of her eye because she turned, and a smile spread across her face.

He raised a hand, giving her a small wave, but still he stood rooted in place, slightly disappointed at her discovery of him.

Taking a deep breath, he pushed through the door. The

warmth and yeasty smell of the bakery stopped him for a second time.

Caroline stopped talking to the girl behind the counter and came to stand next to him. "Good morning, Peter." She glanced at the girl behind the counter and stuttered slightly, "Er, rather, Lord Rockwell."

He stared down at her. They were to be formal on this shopping trip, then. Disappointment pulled down his brow. Was that not to be expected when they were in public?

One corner of her mouth rose slightly higher than the other and she raised a brow at him. He felt warm but didn't know if it was her look or the ovens.

"Lord Rockwell, are you well? You are acting odd this morning."

He swallowed hard and mentally shook himself. What was wrong with him? He was to spend the morning and, if he was lucky, the afternoon with an old friend. What was there not to be happy about? He grinned. "I am well, Lady Caroline. Only struck with a moment of nostalgia. This place has not changed at all since last I was here. It is precisely as I remember it from our childhood years."

Caroline looked around the little shop. "Yes, I believe you will find that true of most of the shops here in Long Compton."

Peter motioned to the girl behind the counter. "Does Mr. Landers still own the shop?"

Caroline followed his gaze and nodded. "Yes. That is his daughter, Miss Sarah Landers. She is of age, you know."

Peter bumped her with his arm. "Do you fancy yourself a bit of a matchmaker, my lady?"

Caroline chuckled. "I thought, perhaps you may need some assistance, as you are already one and thirty and have not yet found a wife." Her face colored to a pretty shade of pink. "But that is not the object of our visit to the village today." She motioned with her head to the shelves of bread lining one of the walls.

Peter walked and looked at the assortment. "Should bread be included in the baskets?"

Caroline nodded. "Yes. Or at least we have always included it."

Peter's stomach grumbled and he patted it. Plucking a baguette from one of the shelves, he took a large bite, then held it out to her.

Caroline shook her head, amusement dancing in her eyes.

Peter swallowed his bite. "If we purchase the bread today, it will be nearly stale by Boxing Day." His brow furrowed.

Caroline chuckled next to him. "You *have* been gone a long time, Lord Rockwell." She motioned back to Miss Landers behind the counter. "We will order the loaves for the baskets today and then Mr. Landers will deliver the bread on the eve of the 25th."

Peter took another bite and nodded. That was logical. Why had he not thought of it? He felt completely out of his element. He turned back to the various breads. "Which kind shall we include?"

Caroline shrugged. "We usually order an assortment, but you can choose whatever you like."

He turned and walked to the opposite side of the store, pointing at the pastries with his baguette. "Shall we order some of these, as well? I believe a cake would be much appreciated."

Caroline grinned. "As I said. That is up to you, my lord. You know your tenants and what their needs are better than I."

Peter grunted and shrugged. He wished such a notion were true. In point of fact, he knew very little of the estate and its tenants. Even the staff were a bit of a mystery to him. He looked at Caroline, suddenly feeling immensely grateful for her assistance. He would be at a loss as to where to even begin on this task. "I believe we shall order cakes, as well."

Caroline nodded and motioned him toward the counter. "Then let us place your order."

He ordered a loaf of bread and a cake for each tenant on the estate before he paid for the baguette he had half-eaten. They walked toward the door and Peter noticed for the first time the footman standing just inside the shop. He pulled the door open, allowing Caroline to exit first, followed by Peter. The footman then followed behind them at a discreet but proper distance.

Peter halted on the walkway. "Do you think we should order a cake for the servants' ball? I know I am not capable of making one."

"Your mother is the one who started the tradition of cooking for the ball at Wirksworth. What did she do about the cake?"

Peter had not thought about his mother's part in the servants' ball in a long time. "She made everything. But I know nothing of how to do such things."

Caroline looked sideways at him. "I believe you shall manage it. Besides, I think they will appreciate the gesture of it more, if it is made by you."

Peter looked at her with wide eyes. "They will not when they taste it, I assure you."

Caroline laughed. "I can help you, if you desire it. We will make sure your servants are not disappointed."

Peter put a hand to his chest. Why was his heart jumping about as it was? After a moment it returned to its normal beat. He took a large, cautious breath. Perhaps he had an abnormality that was only now manifesting itself.

They continued walking. If Caroline helped him with every-thing, it meant they would be spending a great deal of time together. Would her presence be enough to ward off the cold feeling at Wirksworth?

She grinned up at him and he decided she would most

certainly warm up the place. It was good to have friends around him again.

"Now where to, Lady Caroline?" He leaned in a little closer. "Or can I call you Caroline, because there is no one around?"

She shook her head. "I believe it best if we adhere to proprieties while we are in public."

He frowned, feeling suddenly irritated. "As you wish, Lady Caroline." He spoke her name a little louder than necessary, looking around them in an exaggerated manner. He leaned in again. "I believe we are fooling them that we are not more intimately acquainted."

Caroline laughed but covered her mouth with her hand.

They purchased cheese and meat, then pushed into the confectioner's shop. "What sweets shall we buy?"

Caroline put her finger to her lips and tapped.

Peter watched with fascination as her lips pursed and twisted to the side.

"I believe licorice is a must." She picked up several bundles tied with twine and handed them to Peter. He walked over and placed them on the table in front of Mr. Harper.

Caroline moved to another display, picking up sugared almonds and gingerbread. She looked at both and then returned the gingerbread to the stack. She placed cloth bags filled with the candied nuts into Peter's cradled arms before she moved to another display.

"How much candy do you think we need?" Peter truly did not know.

She eyed the multi-colored hard candy. Picking up several bundles in each hand, she turned toward Mr. Harper. "I believe this will be enough."

Peter nodded his head and turned back to Mr. Harper with raised brows. "She believes this should be enough."

Mr. Harper chuckled. "The lady knows what she is about." He counted out the bundles on the table and wrote figures in a ledger to his right. "Did you wish me to send the total on to Wirksworth, my lord?"

Peter nodded. "Please do. I will see you are paid before Christmas."

Mr. Harper smiled. "Thank you, my lord." He tallied the numbers and then tucked the purchases into the large cloth bag Caroline pulled from her reticule. "The village is happy to see you back at Wirksworth, my lord. It has been too long since the Rockwell's were in residence."

Peter slumped slightly. He should not have stayed away so long. He had not intended to, but as time went on, he found he could not return and risk seeing his father and Elizabeth together. Peter bit the inside of his cheek. This man need not hear the reasons and excuses for his long absence. "I am glad to be back, Mr. Harper."

Caroline motioned to the bag on the table and the footman stepped forward and retrieved it.

"Shall we be off?" She looked expectantly at Peter. "We have not yet purchased anything for the servants."

Peter grunted. "Ugh. And I thought deciding what we put in the baskets was difficult. I have no notion what to buy for the servants."

Caroline patted his arm. "In truth, most of the servants would be happy with a few coins."

Peter grinned. "Then we are done."

Caroline laughed as she shook her head. "Oh, no. You are not going to get out of it that easily. Mrs. Harris and Porter should receive something more personal. Something you have taken more thought in picking." She nudged him in the side with her elbow. "Although, I am sure they would appreciate the coins with the gift." She looked down the road at the rows of shops. "What are their likes?"

Peter shrugged. "How should I know such things? I have been away for years." He looked down at her. "And if I am being honest, I was not so concerned about the servants before I left." His cheeks burned with the admission.

They came to a book shop and Caroline stopped in front of it. "Do either of them like to read?"

Peter shrugged. "I already told you; I have no idea."

She gave him a look of exaggerated annoyance. "Let us look and see if there is anything that, perhaps, they may like."

They stood in front of the shelves, each looking at the spines of the books before them. Peter sighed. What did they hope to find in here? He glanced over at Caroline and took a step to the side, bringing him closer to her. The smell of lilac drifted past his nose. He breathed in deeply, his eyes skittering across the spines, but his brain registering little. Had she always smelled of lilacs? He doubted it. Perfumes were the markings of a lady already out in society, not a little girl.

"Have you ever seen either of them reading?" Caroline looked up at him, frustration lacing her voice.

He shook his head. "No. But as I said, *I have been away*." He emphasized the last words, because apparently, she had not heard them the first few times he had said them.

Caroline gave him a bland look. "Really? I had not noticed."

Peter put a hand to his heart. "You wound me, my lady. I have believed all these years that you were devastated by my departure. Indeed, I was convinced it was the reason you were not yet married—because you could not get over my leaving." He sighed dramatically. "Now I find you did not even notice I had gone."

Her face seemed pinker than it had moments ago. Peter looked around, so as to keep himself from staring at her. She looked lovely with the added color. He cleared his throat. She was, no doubt, embarrassed by his loud performance.

He looked back to the bookshelf in front of him. A title caught his eye and he reached forward, pulling it from the shelf. He rubbed his fingers across the title, *Histories or Tales of Past Times* by M. Perrault.

Caroline looked over at the book. "Fairy tales? For whom are you considering that book?"

Peter opened the book and looked at the picture inside the front cover. Several noblemen and women sat in front of a fireplace with an old woman, who was obviously telling them tales. Mother Goose's Tales was displayed on a plaque on the wall above their heads.

"Mrs. Harris read these to Eleanor and me as children." Memories of nights in the nursery with Mrs. Harris assaulted him.

Caroline gently took the book from his hands, studying it. "Yes, I think I remember she read it to me on one occasion. But then the book was lost, and she was not able to finish the story we had started."

Peter took the book. "It was my fault the book disappeared." His chest tightened as the afternoon in the nursery all those years ago came back to his mind as if it were yesterday. "Eleanor had taken my toy soldier and refused to give it back. She raised it above her head, and I was unable to jump high enough to reach it. When she ran away from me, I grabbed the book from the table and threw it at her." He continued to rub at the letters pressed into the leather. "I missed Eleanor, but the book landed in the fireplace. It was an old book and the spine was ragged. It caught fire immediately. All I could do was watch as it burned away."

Caroline laid her hand on his arm. "I'm sorry, Peter. Was Mrs. Harris angry when she learned what happened?"

Peter shook his head. "I never told her and neither did

Eleanor. She knew she was partly to blame. When Mrs. Harris asked after the book, we pretended we did not know where it was."

Caroline gave him a small nudge. "I believe you have found the perfect gift for Mrs. Harris."

Peter shook his head. "But if I give her this, I shall have to admit to what I did."

Caroline raised her eyes to his. "Not necessarily. You could tell her you didn't remember her finding the book." Her voice lowered. "But would it be so terrible if you confessed your part in its disappearance? It was a long time ago and the actions of a young boy. You are a man now."

She was right and he knew it. Why was he trying to take the coward's way out? He bristled. He had never thought himself one, until now.

He moved over toward the proprietor of the shop and placed the book on the counter. "You are right, Lady Caroline." He waited while the man wrapped the book in brown paper and tied it with twine. He asked for the bill to be sent to Wirksworth and picked up the parcel.

"It is time for me to make this mistake right. I only hope I am not too late, and she can forgive me." He hoped his stomach would stop churning before Boxing Day arrived.

C aroline lingered by the stacks as Peter finished up with his purchase. She pulled a large book from the shelf in front of her and opened it up. A map covered the whole of the page, pale colors dividing the country of France into smaller parts. Peter stepped up behind her and leaned in close.

She shivered.

He reached into his pocket and withdrew a pair of spectacles. Placing them on his nose, he reached around her and touched the dot marking Lyon with his index finger.

Caroline gaped at him. Never had she seen a man look so handsome in spectacles.

"I lived here for nearly a year." His arm pressed against hers.

She closed her mouth and shifted back against him slightly. "What did you do there for so long?"

Peter shrugged. "Studied."

Caroline turned her head to the side so she could see his face better. "You did not get enough of that at Cambridge?"

He set his package on the table next to them and pulled the

book into his hands. His fingers brushed over hers, as he took the book from her. She nearly closed her eyes as the warmth spread up her arms and into her chest. Why must he have this effect on her even after all these years? She was a lady now, not some doe-eyed girl in love with her brother's best friend.

"I met a man, a Monsieur Babineaux. He was an architect of great prominence. He took me in, and I became his student for a time. Became a part of his family."

Caroline's head tilted to the side as she listened. "Why? I never knew you to be interested in architecture."

"Why not?" Peter shrugged again. "I did not know I enjoyed the subject until I began to speak with Monsieur Babineaux. I had learned long before that to learn at the feet of those renowned for a specific gift was a rare occasion. Why should I not accept when presented with the chance?"

Caroline nodded. "I suppose I can understand your reasoning. When would you ever have such an opportunity again?"

Peter smiled, but the sparkle in his eyes which usually accompanied it was absent. Was he only telling her part of his story?

Caroline chided herself. Why did she feel he owed her all of his secrets?

"Is that what you did at every place you visited? Stayed and learned of something new?"

Peter's head nodded slowly. "In most places. Some I stayed only a short time, but there were many that offered me knowledge I could never fully get from a book."

He thumbed through several pages, his face softening as he ran his fingers over several of the outlines of various countries.

Caroline swallowed, feeling as though she was interrupting a private moment. "Are you to purchase this book as well?"

He snapped the book shut with a pop, placing it back on the shelf. "No. I am not here to increase my own library, but to find gifts for the servants. Perhaps I will return after the holidays and purchase it."

Caroline licked her lips. "But what if someone should buy it before you are able to return?"

Peter removed his spectacles and tucked them inside his coat pocket. He extended his arm out to her. "Then it is not to be mine." He motioned toward the door.

Caroline put her hand on his arm and let him lead her from the shop. As she passed over the threshold, she cast a glance over her shoulder, committing to memory the location of the book.

They wandered about several other shops, but Peter did not see anything he thought appropriate for his long-time butler.

He stopped in front of the bakery again and opened the door for her. "Shall we stop for tea before we journey home?"

Caroline's stomach rumbled.

Peter grinned. "I shall take that as a yes."

He found them a small table in the corner of the bakery by the window. Afternoon sunlight streamed in, warming Caroline.

A young girl approached the table. "May I bring you tea, Lady Caroline?"

"Yes. Thank you, Sarah." Caroline smiled up at the girl, who turned to Peter.

"And for you, sir?"

Peter leaned toward her. "You would not happen to have chocolate, would you?"

Sarah nodded her head. "We do, sir."

Peter grinned. "Wonderful. Please bring the cream and sugar also. Then I should like to have chocolate and an apricot biscuit." He looked at Caroline. "What shall you have with your tea, Lady Caroline?"

"No tea?" She had never had chocolate. Her friend, Harriette, had told her of the one time she had tried it. Harriette said it was very bitter and tasted of burned coffee.

"I drank chocolate almost every morning while in New Spain. It is a drink they have consumed for hundreds of years."

Caroline traced over a scratch in the table with her finger. Sitting here with Peter, chocolate felt so exotic, so *not her*. She turned to Sarah. "I shall have the same as Lord Rockwell, Sarah."

Sarah's brow furrowed, and she cast a worried look at Peter. "I beg your pardon, my lord."

Peter waved away her apology.

Sarah turned her gaze back to Caroline. "Even the chocolate, my lady?"

Caroline nodded, even as her stomach churned. Whether it was from hunger or trepidation over the chocolate, she was not sure.

Sarah dipped her head, first to Peter and then to Caroline. "I'll return in a moment, my lord. My Lady." She left them, disappearing behind a curtain at the rear of the shop.

"You spent time in New Spain?" Caroline's mouth twitched to the side. What kind of a question was that? Had he not already stated that he had gone to New Spain? Why could she not manage to act like the near four and twenty years old that she was?

Peter drummed his fingers on the tabletop and nodded his head. "Yes, nearly a year."

Caroline's mouth dropped open in a most unladylike fashion. Her mother would be appalled, should she be here. But she was not, so Caroline discreetly closed it.

Peter's gaze dropped from her eyes, focusing for a moment on her lips. Without thinking, she licked them, quickly pulling her tongue back inside her mouth when she realized what she was doing. She bit her lip instead.

Why was he looking at her in such a way? It was likely due to

her untoward behavior. What kind of lady acted as she did in front
of a gentleman? She knew how to act and had done so for years.
Why, when Peter was around, could she not manage to act in the
proper way she had been taught?

One side of Peter's brow rose slowly.

Releasing her lip, Caroline cleared her throat and Peter's gaze
flicked back up to hers. Had his face pinked slightly or was it just a
reflection from the sunlight?

"Whatever did you find to do for the whole of a year?"
Speaking of his travels seemed the safest course of action.

His face pulled into an easy smile and he leaned back in his
chair. "A great many things, actually. I learned about extracting
silver ore from the ground. While I never actually mined it, I did
get to oversee production for most of the year I was there."

Sarah placed a cup and saucer in front of each of them. A
bitter, burned smell wafted to her nose. Caroline looked down into
the cup of dark brown liquid and wrinkled her nose. She lifted her
eyes to Peter's.

He grinned even wider and poured a little cream into his cup,
stirring his drink.

Caroline leaned over the table and looked down into his cup.
The dark liquid was now a lighter brown. She sat back slightly,
and Peter nudged the creamer toward her. "I learned in the West
Indies to add a little cream. It makes it taste better."

Caroline poured a small amount into her cup, stirring and
mixing them together. Hers was not as light as Peter's so she added
a little more.

Resting her spoon against her saucer, she lifted the cup to her
lips, taking a small sip. Her nose wrinkled again as she lowered the
cup and coughed. The cream had only served to lessen the bitter
taste slightly.

She glanced up and noticed Peter staring at her. His cup

remained on the table, his lips twitching as if he were holding back a laugh.

Caroline pursed her lips together. "Why are you laughing at me? I do not see you drinking this abhorrent drink."

Peter pulled the sugar jar closer to him and without lifting his gaze from her face, placed two spoonfuls of sugar into his drink. He raised a brow as he stirred purposefully.

After a moment, he placed his spoon to the side and lifted the cup to his mouth. His eyes closed and he looked to be savoring the taste on his tongue.

Caroline pulled the sugar closer and added the same amount as Peter had, to her chocolate. She also added a bit more cream. Mixing it all together, she lifted the cup tentatively to her lips. The sweet taste flooded her senses and she felt her eyes close. It was no wonder he had been unable to continue laughing at her. Such was not to be endured when something so delicious was within reach.

Peter's quiet chuckle sounded from across the table. "Am I to guess you have reconsidered your original opinion of chocolate?"

Caroline took one more sip before she returned her cup to the saucer. She nodded her head and ran her tongue over her lips to get any remaining drink.

Again, Peter seemed unable to look at anywhere else.

She took a handkerchief from her reticule and dabbed at her lips. "Do I have chocolate on my face?"

Peter shook his head and picked up his cup again. "No. Your face is lovely."

Caroline swallowed hard. Had he just said he thought her pretty? Or was he just saying what he believed he ought to say to a lady? His brow furrowed and she knew he had not meant what he said.

Peter dipped the corner of his biscuit into the chocolate before taking a large bite.

Caroline's eyes widened and her mouth twitched.

Peter chuckled, then started to cough. He lifted the serviette to his mouth as tears filled his eyes and he continued to cough. He took a drink of his chocolate and the coughing slowed. He cleared his throat several times, then looked up at her with narrowed eyes. "Must you have laughed? You might well have killed me from choking on the biscuit crumbs."

Caroline put her hand to her mouth, tears now filling her eyes as well. "I beg your pardon, my lord. I did not intend to kill you."

Peter shook his head, still eying her suspiciously. "Imagine surviving all those years of traveling, only to meet my demise at the hand of a young lady and a biscuit."

Caroline let out one last laugh and Peter joined her. Several people in the shop turned to stare at them, but Caroline avoided their gazes. This was her time with Peter, and she did not intend to let anyone interrupt.

"My parents would dispute your claim." She lifted her cup to her lips and dropped her gaze to it. Why had she brought up such a topic when the one they had been discussing was so pleasant?

"Which claim is that?" Peter looked at her with amused eyes.

Now was her chance. He did not know to what she had been referring. She thought and tried to grasp anything else from their conversation that her parents could possibly find exception with. She could think of nothing.

He leaned back into his seat again; one hand had dropped out of sight beneath the table and the other fidgeted with his saucer, twisting it around and around. He said nothing, just waited for her to reply.

"It is nothing. I should not have mentioned it." The more he scrutinized her, the warmer she became. Oh, curse her thoughtless replies. She had not always been this way. Or at least not for the last several years. Mother had seen to it before her come out. But for some reason, of late she had taken to speaking whatever entered her mind. Caroline sighed. It must be her discontent in chaperoning reckless young ladies.

Peter lifted his hand from his saucer and waggled his finger at her. "Oh, no. You do not get off so easily, Lady Caroline. I can see it in those lovely blue eyes of yours, that you have something to say."

Again, he had called her lovely. Well, not her precisely, but her eyes. And if one's eyes were lovely, did that not mean the rest of her was lovely also? Caroline nearly guffawed out loud at that absurd thought.

"What would the marquess and his wife have to dispute with me over?"

Caroline tilted her head to the side. "Can we not forget I ever said anything?"

Peter shook his head. "We cannot. I find I can think of nothing else, now. I shall not have a moment's peace until I know."

"Very well." Caroline's agitation punctuated her words. When she returned home, she must recite *I will think before I speak* no less than a hundred times. Perhaps then she would remember to hold her tongue in the future. "You asserted that a *young* lady was nearly responsible for your demise."

Peter nodded and stared at her expectantly.

"It is the *young* part which would cause my parents to disagree. They do not consider me young by any notion and quite vocally have placed me on the shelf."

Peter sat forward; his brow creased. "What? How could that be true you cannot yet be more than—" He looked to the ceiling as if thinking, "twenty years old."

"I shall be four and twenty come February." She ducked her head slightly. "I am very nearly a spinster."

47

Peter shook his head. She was not sure he had even heard what she had said.

"Your parents are old fashioned and quickly becoming relics of the past."

Caroline let out a soft chuckle. "You have been away too long and experienced too many different cultures. I am afraid Mama and Papa are in the majority in their thinking."

"Well, it is absurd," Peter mumbled. He shoved the last of his biscuit into his mouth and chewed exaggeratedly. When at last his mouth was free of food, he smirked at her. "I stand by my previous statement." He motioned to her plate. "Are you finished eating?"

Caroline looked at her half-eaten biscuit. She nodded, feeling slightly guilty for leaving any food behind when she knew there were so many people in England who went hungry each night. "I should like to get some bread to take with me before I leave."

Peter stood and walked the short distance to her chair. Helping her to stand, he nodded his head. "I have no place to be. I can wait and then see you home after."

Caroline shook her head. "I told you I have other shopping to do. You need not see me home."

His smile dropped. Could it be he was as disappointed as she that their time together was coming to an end? "But, we would be honored if you would join us at Whitley for the evening."

He smiled and Caroline thought her knees may give out.

"I should be delighted." He motioned to the shelves of bread and put his hand on the small of her back, guiding her toward them. Caroline closed her eyes as the heat from his hand warmed her inside and out. Truly, she would be happy if this was even a little of what her life could be like.

She stumbled on a raised floor plank and jerked her eyes open again. What was she doing? Putting her feelings and emotions toward Peter on display for the whole of the village to see?

Peter's hand moved from her back and now looped around her side. "Are you well?" he whispered into her ear.

No, she was not well. She could hardly breathe. Her heart felt as though it might pound out of her chest and her head was feeling hazy. She was not well at all. But she could not tell Peter any of those things. He would question her and surely send for Doctor Hastings. Caroline did not need a doctor. She needed space.

She stepped out of his grasp and grabbed hold of several loaves of bread. "I am well. I only forgot to step over that floorboard. My mind is elsewhere, I am afraid."

Peter clasped his empty hands in front of him. "I understand completely. There is still so much to do before Christmas and Boxing day."

"Yes, so much to do." She echoed his words, her voice quiet. Her head lowered and she focused on the loaves in her hands.

"Do you need assistance back to your carriage?"

Caroline shook her head. "No. Thomas is just outside the door waiting for me. He will take my parcels."

Peter tipped his hat. "Then I shall bid you good day. Until this evening, Lady Caroline."

She stood still, staring at the shelves full of baguettes. When she heard the tinkle of the bell on the door, her shoulders sagged, and she breathed in deeply. How was it possible to both crave and dread another person's company?

Caroline pushed thoughts of Peter from her mind and focused on the biscuits and other pastries in the shop.

Sarah boxed up all of Caroline's purchases and tied them up with twine. Thomas stepped into the shop and Sarah began to load him down with the boxes. "Thank you, Sarah. Please give your parents my regards." Caroline offered the girl a little wave as she walked through the door Thomas held open.

They arrived at the carriage and Thomas began to place the boxes inside.

Caroline placed a hand on his arm. "Wait, Thomas."

The footman stopped and turned his head toward her.

"I have some more shopping to do. I wondered if you might do me a favor?"

Thomas nodded. "Of course, my lady."

Caroline pointed to the stack of boxes. "Would you please deliver these to Harker Street? One loaf and one box to each house."

Thomas's eyes widened. "Harker Street, my lady?"

Caroline nodded. "Yes. If you run out, please let me know how many more are needed, and we shall see they are delivered tomorrow."

Thomas nodded.

She had specifically asked for Thomas to accompany her because of his large size. He was tall and very muscular. He would be safe delivering the parcels to Harker Street. While it was not as dangerous as many streets in London, there was still an element of danger.

He removed his livery, wearing only his shirt. He looked down at himself and grimaced.

Caroline placed a hand on his arm. "Thank you, Thomas."

He nodded again. "My pleasure, my lady." He deposited the last few parcels into the carriage. "Let me see you home and then I shall see to these."

Caroline shook her head. "I have a few more presents I have yet to buy. You go and deliver the packages and then return and fetch me. Harker Street is not far off. You should have no trouble getting these delivered before I am finished with my shopping."

Thomas's brow furrowed. "But my lady, it would not be proper to leave you unattended."

Caroline raised a brow at the man. "I shall be well, Thomas. It is not as if we are in Town. This is Long Compton. I will be safe. I shall keep to the main street shops, if that will make you happy." She shooed him away. "Now, hurry along."

Thomas walked a few steps forward. "Who am I to say the deliveries are from, my lady? The Marquess of Killingsworth?"

Caroline scrunched her face to one side as she thought. For some reason, she did not wish her parents or her brother and his wife to get the credit for the packages, nor did she care to get the credit herself. "Just tell them it is from Father Christmas." She turned to leave, but a thought struck her. What good was some food if their houses were cold?

Caroline turned back. "Oh, Thomas, please see that each house gets a bucket of coal, as well."

Thomas opened his mouth, but Caroline held up her hand to ward off his protestations. "Tell Mr. Luster I will stop by on my way home and pay him for the coal."

Thomas sighed heavily but nodded. "Yes, my lady."

Caroline gave him a satisfied smile. "Come fetch me when you are finished." She turned on her heel, not waiting to hear if he had any further questions or objections.

First, she stopped at the milliner's shop and picked out several lovely ribbons and pieces of lace for Lydia. They would pair well with the carved hand mirror she had found on her way back from London.

Caroline left the shop and walked down the street. She stopped in front of the tobacco shop. A finely carved ivory snuff box was displayed. It was the perfect gift for her father, but she already had a book for him she had purchased in London. Caroline tilted her head, studying the case. It was no matter. She could give her father this as well. Perhaps she would keep this and give it to him for Epiphany.

As she exited the shop, she nearly ran into a woman on the walk. The woman was great with child and held the hand of a little girl. Both were dressed in ragged clothes and neither had a coat. The pink tinge of their cheeks and hands indicated the coldness of their bodies.

Caroline's heart broke for the woman. She removed her heavy cloak and placed it about the woman's shoulders. The woman moved to refuse it, offering protests, but Caroline waved them away with a smile. She handed her fur lined muff to the little girl, who accepted it with wide eyes.

A bitter breeze blew past, bringing tears to Caroline's eyes. The woman again made to remove the cloak. Caroline shook her head, instead pressing coins into the woman's hand. "Buy some food for your family."

Before another wind could suck her breath away, Caroline turned and quickly walked back to the book shop. She made her way to the shelves she and Peter had been perusing. She found the map book and flipped it open again. It opened to a map of India. Had Peter ever been to India? She guessed he had. It seemed he had been about everywhere in his time away from England. Oh, what he must have seen and learned.

She turned to the map of France again. Peter had mentioned he had lived in France for nearly a year. Was it there he met the lady he had brought to England to marry? He must love her very much if he went to the trouble of moving her here from France.

Caroline snapped the book shut. Was it proper to buy a book for a man engaged to another woman? She bit her lip. He had looked so longingly at the book; she knew he desired it. Caroline took it to the counter. What was so improper about buying a gift for a friend?

"Find something else you were interested in, my lady?" the shopkeeper asked.

Caroline smiled. "Yes, but it is to be a surprise. If the gentleman you saw with me earlier comes looking for this book, please be so kind as to not reveal it was I who purchased it. I wish it to be a surprise for Epiphany."

The older man smiled kindly. "Of course, my lady."

"Thank you." She placed the money on the counter and waited as he finished tying the package with twine.

Her stomach fluttered with a combination of excitement and nerves at the thought of giving this to Peter.

❧ 6 ❧

Peter checked himself in the mirror one last time.

"Is everything to your satisfaction, my lord?" His valet brushed at Peter's shoulder.

Peter straightened his waist coat and nodded. "Yes, Jennings. Thank you."

He strode from the room and headed down the stairway. When he reached the bottom, he waited for Porter to finish his instructions with Carter.

The butler shooed Carter away and stepped into the entry-way. "Good morning, my lord."

"Porter, please see that the sled is readied. I will be needing it after breakfast. We will be fetching the yule log and other greenery to adorn these great halls."

The butler smiled, as much as he ever did. "It will be a welcome sight, my lord. It has been some time since Wirksworth has felt the holiday spirit."

Peter's throat tightened as he thought on the last time he

remembered the house celebrating any kind of holiday. It was the year before his mother had died.

He pushed his emotions back. Now was not the time to dwell on them. He needed to eat quickly and then make his way over to Whitley Wood. He had sent a note to Caroline asking her to help him. She had replied immediately.

If Peter were being honest with himself, he was excited to have Caroline along with him. While things were different now than when they had been children, he still enjoyed her company very much. So much so, he had not dwelled on Miss Tree and her identity for any of the time they were together. Or at least, for most of the time.

There had been a point in the conversation at the bakery yesterday when Peter had questioned if Caroline would like Miss Tree. He had thought on it more last evening after he returned home from supper at Whitley Wood. He had concluded that she would. Caroline and Miss Tree seemed to have similar characteristics. Granted, Peter did not really know much of Miss Tree's character. But from what he did know, it seemed to him they would get on quite well.

He grunted. He supposed he should have asked Montjoy and his wife to accompany them. Peter missed those days long ago when there was no need for propriety. When they were just children and they spent time together without decorum constantly looming over them.

But they were not children anymore. One look at Caroline reminded him of that fact, as did the warmth in his face and chest.

He entered the breakfast room and dished several eggs and a thick slice of ham onto his plate. He scooped up a few slices of bread on his way past, setting them atop his ham. He sat down at the table and buttered his bread in silence.

Taking a bite, he looked around. The silence was nearly suffocating.

He swallowed, and it caught in his throat. The notion that he needed to marry and bring some life back into this house was all the more evident now. Was Miss Tree the one who would fill that role? His jaw tightened, pinching his lips shut. How could he know for certain if he did not even know her? He slammed his hand on the table. But he did know her, or she had implied as much. *If you cannot remember, I shall not be the one to tell you.*

A pair of lovely blue eyes drifted to his mind. At first, he thought they were Miss Tree's, because that is whom he was thinking on. But they reminded him of Caroline. Which was not a wholly unpleasant thought, either.

He had always enjoyed Caroline's company when they were children, but since returning to Long Compton, his feelings had become more complicated.

No longer were they fishing in the pond or playing Robin Hood in the forest. Peter smiled to himself. Did Caroline play Robin Hood anymore? He knew it was doubtful she still climbed trees or swung from a rope to rescue a captured knight. The thought saddened him.

He pushed his plate back. Today he would spend the day with her. His muscles felt tense and jumpy.

Anxious to get his day started, he pushed back from the table and moved out of the breakfast room.

Porter fetched Peter's beaver and greatcoat. "Please see that the fires in the south parlor and the great hall are stoked. I want the rooms warm so as to allow the greenery to relax once we get back. It will make it easier to decorate with it around the staircases."

"Yes, my lord." Porter helped slip the greatcoat over Peter's shoulders. "Will Lady Caroline be returning with you? Shall I have Mrs. Pratt prepare tea?"

Peter nodded. "Yes. Although, I believe Lord and Lady Montjoy will also be with us."

Porter nodded. "I shall inform Mrs. Pratt and see things are ready when you return."

Peter placed his beaver on his head and turned toward the door. "Thank you, Porter."

Peter stepped out onto the snow-covered drive and turned toward the stables just as his team of horses was led out with the sled hitched up behind them. James brought them to where Peter stood.

Peter looked the sled over. It looked so much smaller than he remembered. He had only been fifteen or sixteen the last time he and his mother had taken it out.

He ran a hand over the shiny wooden side. "You have taken good care of her. I should never have guessed it would look so fine. Thank you."

James grinned. He was missing more teeth than when Peter had left, but he was still the same, kindhearted man. It was why he was such a good stable master. He showed the same kindness to man and beast.

"Warm bricks have been placed on the floor, beneath the rugs, my lord."

"Just as thorough as you always were, James."

Peter stepped up into the sled and flicked the reins. The sled smoothly set into motion, traveling down the drive.

He turned onto the lane leading up to Whitley Wood, the castle barely visible. It was an impressive structure. He had often been jealous of Montjoy as a boy. After all, what boy did not wish to live in a castle?

He maneuvered the sled over the draw bridge. The water in the moat had a covering of ice. Snow drifted up against the base of the castle walls. He pulled through the hollow in the keep, stopping the sled in the interior courtyard.

Peter hopped from the driver's box and forced himself to slow his steps as he approached the front entrance. He knocked and the butler quickly opened the door. "Good morning to you, Lord Rockwell."

"And to you, Stanton." Peter straightened his waistcoat. "Would Lord Montjoy and Lady Caroline be about?"

The butler opened the door wider. "Lady Caroline is expecting you. Please, follow me."

Stanton led Peter into a pale pink room. Lady Caroline and Lady Montjoy sat next to the fireplace, each working on a stitchery.

Peter's brow furrowed. He never thought of Caroline as one fond of stitchery. It seemed far too sedate of an activity with little knowledge gained from it.

Caroline scowled down at the fabric in her hands, her needle picking at something. Peter smiled. That seemed more like the Caroline he remembered.

Stanton announced Peter and her head jerked up, the sampler dropping to her lap. Was she happy to see him or simply relieved she need not struggle with the sewing any longer?

She smiled and stood up to greet him.

"Sit down, Caroline. You are not mistress of this house. It is not your responsibility to greet our guest." Lady Killingsworth's voice sounded from the opposite side of the room.

Caroline's head drooped and she sat back in her chair, picking up the sewing once again. Her mouth worked, as if she were talking to herself, and she yanked at the obviously knotted thread.

Lady Killingsworth stood and walked smoothly toward Peter. "Lord Rockwell. How are you this morning?"

Peter bowed over the lady's hand. "Very well, my lady." His eyes flicked to Caroline briefly. She seemed such a different person when she was here with her mother. It was as if someone snuffed out the light that glowed only outside her mother's watchful eye.

He returned his gaze back to Lady Killingsworth. "I am come to see if Lord and Lady Montjoy," he looked back to Caroline, "and Lady Caroline would care to accompany me into the forest to obtain greenery and a yule log. Wirksworth is in great need of some holiday cheer after all of these years."

Caroline glanced up, but quickly returned her gaze to the fabric in front of her. Peter guessed she was trying to appear uninterested for her mother's benefit, or at least he hoped that was the reason.

Lady Montjoy stood and walked over. "I can speak for Lord Montjoy and myself. We would love to join you." She glanced to Lady Killingsworth. "If it is acceptable to you, my lady?"

Lady Killingsworth nodded. "Yes, it is acceptable. I am in no mood to go traipsing about the forest looking for mistletoe and holly. That is a chore for the young. Which I am not, anymore." She ran a hand over her hair, indicating she did not believe her own words.

Peter glanced at Caroline. Her eyes were focused on the stitchery in her hands, but he could tell she was listening intently to the conversation. Her needle moved very little. Did her interest in the conversation mean she wished to go with him? Or was it more out of annoyance that she would be forced to do so? Her reply to his note had simply said yes, she was available to accompany him. The response left much for interpretation.

"Go ahead, all of you." Lady Killingsworth eyed her daughter-in-law, "but you shall have the responsibility of putting up all the decorations, my dear, so I recommend you make haste. I am much too tired for that chore. I am sure Mrs. Glover and some of the maids would be willing to assist you." The countess glanced at Caroline who still seemed intent on her stitchery, although it was only an act, Peter could tell. "Caroline. Put down that sewing. Have you learned no better manners than to ignore our guest, especially when he has been so kind as to single you out to accompany him?"

Had Lady Killingsworth always been this harsh and demanding? Peter tried to think back but could remember very little of her from their childhood years.

"Begging your pardon, Lord Rockwell." Caroline stood and curtsied, but her eyes stayed trained on a spot on the carpet in front of her. "I should be honored to accompany you. Thank you for the offer." Her mouth continued to move. He thought he heard her mutter something about not being singled out if Samuel and Lydia were also invited.

Caroline glanced up quickly at her mother, obviously ensuring her last words had not been overheard. The countess had turned away and was speaking to Lady Montjoy.

Peter's brow furrowed. He did not like seeing Caroline like this. He missed her vibrant and fun character.

Lady Killingsworth turned toward the door. "The menus are in need of my attention." She turned her head and glanced at Caroline. "Do dress sensibly, today, Caroline. It is winter, after all."

Caroline nodded mutely.

What was that about? Did Lady Killingsworth not think her daughter of three and twenty capable of dressing appropriately?

Lady Killingsworth breezed from the room, leaving Peter alone with Caroline and Lady Montjoy.

He looked to Caroline, but either she refused to look at him or was too embarrassed by her mother's insinuations. He stared at the crown of her bent head.

Lady Montjoy cleared her throat. "Why do I not fetch Lord Montjoy and my pelisse while Lady Caroline fetches hers? We can meet back here shortly."

Peter glanced over to Lady Montjoy. "That sounds like a grand plan."

Caroline raised her eyes and the pink tint to her cheeks answered his question.

Peter frowned. How could a mother treat her daughter in such a manner? And in front of guests, no less. Perhaps if she spent the day at Wirksworth he would get time with the Caroline he had seen yesterday in the village.

She swished past him as she left the room to fetch warmer clothes.

Montjoy was the first to arrive back in the parlor. He strode into the room and immediately sought Peter out. They shook hands and Montjoy smacked him on the shoulder with his other hand. "I am in your debt, my friend." He looked about the room, as if ensuring they were alone. "I thought Lady Montjoy may be driven to bedlam, should she have to spend another day in full with my mother. I am sure you recall how demanding she can be."

Peter smiled. "It is funny, but I do not remember those parts of our childhood." He smiled. "But I am glad to be of service."

As if on cue, Lady Montjoy and Caroline walked through the doorway. "Did I hear my name?" Lady Montjoy asked.

"I was just thanking Rockwell for thinking of this glorious idea. I think we are all ready for an outing. Do you not agree, my dear?"

The lady smiled at her husband.

Was theirs an arranged marriage or a love match? Peter

conceded that even after watching them, he still did not know. They seemed to get along well enough, but he did not detect any true partiality on either of their parts.

Peter held his arm out to Caroline. She had not only added a heavy wool pelisse, but it looked as if she had changed into a heavy wool dress as well. She was not leaving anything for her mother to grouse about. "Are you ready, my lady?"

She nodded her head and put her hand on his arm. He led her out of the room and down the corridor.

As they moved into the entryway, Peter leaned in close and whispered into her ear, "You look very warm, Caroline."

Her eyes flicked up to his and he smiled.

Her brow furrowed.

Gah, did she think he was mocking her?

He patted her gloved hand. "And may I add, very lovely."

A tiny smile formed on her lips.

Peter's chest rose slightly. He had never wished so hard for a smile so slight in his life.

Once outside, he helped her onto the seat next to him, while Samuel situated Lady Montjoy on the bench behind.

"You can sit in the back with us, if it is too cold in the driver's seat." Montjoy looked pointedly at his sister.

Caroline shook her head. "No, thank you, Samuel. I find I prefer the view up here."

He stood rooted in place. "It is not as if that seat is so very much higher. The view cannot be so different than it is back here." There was a hardness in his tone.

"And yet, I still prefer it." There was an equal hardness in Caroline's voice.

Curious.

Montjoy glared at his sister, but when she stayed firmly in place, he settled in next to his wife.

Peter shrugged and flicked the reins, sending the horses cantering down the small walking path they used to travel between estates. The runners of the sled were much wider than the path, but with the snow on the ground it did not matter.

Caroline sat beside him and the day seemed full of promise.

❦ 7 ❦

The sun glinted off the snow crystals creating a sparkling scene before them.

Peter stopped the sled at the edge of the forest which straddled Wirksworth and Whitley Wood. A second sled, which was a wagon fitted with sled runners, was already waiting for them. Several footmen stood waiting beside it.

Peter jumped down from the box and held out his hand to help Caroline. He looked up at her and smiled as she stepped down.

Once she was securely on the ground, he released her hand and moved to the back of the sled, pulling two axes from the straps on the rear seatback. Peter handed one to Samuel and kept the other for himself. He then withdrew a long saw with a handle on each end from the box that ran along the underside of the sled. That one he handed to a nearby footman. "How do we want to do this, Montjoy? Shall we stay together or divide and conquer?"

Peter stepped closer to Caroline and she grinned up at him.

Samuel cleared his throat. His eyes flicked between Caroline and Peter, a scowl turning down the corners of his mouth.

"I believe it best if we stay together." His words came out through gritted teeth.

Peter nodded; his brow slightly creased. "Very well. Where shall we begin our search?"

Lydia stepped forward. "We will need a lot of greenery so if we can find a big enough yule log, we can strip the branches off. It will give us the greenery and the log at the same time."

Samuel still eyed his sister. Caroline returned his looks with equal firmness.

"It sounds like a logical plan. Let us start walking. Shout out if you see a tree you think large enough." Peter held his arm out to Caroline.

She placed her hand on his arm, but he moved her hand, tucking it into the crook of his elbow. "There are bound to be some roots and branches hidden beneath the snow that we cannot readily see. Perhaps it would be best if you held on."

Caroline tightened her hold and nodded her head, but only because she did not think she could form words. He may only be doing this out of protection, but still she felt the closeness and it made her giddy.

They moved through the trees, the crunching of the snow beneath their feet the only sound to break the silence of the forest.

"Is there still the holly patch on the north end?" Peter looked straight ahead.

"Yes. It has expanded greatly in the past few years. We should be able to obtain all we need."

"And what of the mistletoe?" Peter grinned and nudged Caroline gently with his shoulder.

Her face burned against the cold. "It is scattered throughout the trees. You need only look up, in most cases." Both their eyes turned upwards, looking into the branches above them.

Nothing was there but evergreens. Disappointment and relief flooded through her. But what if there had been mistletoe? Would he have kissed her there in the forest or would he have rejected her? Would he even like to kiss her?

With Samuel and Lydia right behind them, the notion seemed unlikely, even *if* he was interested in an arrangement with her. Which he surely was not.

The silence now felt awkward and uncomfortable.

Samuel spoke up from behind. "What of that tree up ahead?" He came up next to Peter and pointed at a tree in the distance.

Peter picked up his pace, forcing Caroline to walk faster to keep up. He walked around the tree, running his hand over the bark and circling the trunk. "Yes, Montjoy. I think you found a perfect one. It is just the right size and it has plenty of branches for us to shear off and use on the tables and staircases."

He called the footman over, exchanging the axe for the saw. "Well, Montjoy, shall we do this ourselves? Just as we did when we were boys?"

Samuel nodded, his grin covering the entirety of his face.

Peter put a hand on Caroline's arm, moving her gently back several steps. "Please stay back. I do not wish for you to be injured."

Samuel brought Lydia over to stand next to Caroline. "I believe they think us either small children or quite daft with the way they are fussing." Caroline smiled at Lydia.

Caroline would never say it out loud, but she was thrilled Peter would care about her enough to worry over her safety.

Peter and Samuel worked the saw together until at last the tree toppled to the ground. The footmen stepped forward, moving toward the felled tree.

Caroline did not envy them their task of trying to get the large log back to the sled. The footmen began to strip the branches from the trunk, laying them on a canvas rug in a pile.

Peter returned to Caroline's side. "They can see to this tree; let us continue the search for the Wirksworth yule log and perhaps a Tannenbaum."

Caroline looked up at him. "A tannom what?"

Peter chuckled. "Tannenbaum. It is a tree for Christmas. I learned of them when I was living at Westphalia."

"What is a Christmas tree?" Caroline asked.

"It is a tree, such as these, which is cut down and then taken indoors and decorated with candles and other decorations. Princess Caroline puts one up in the royal palace every Christmas."

Caroline looked at him with doubtful eyes. "You plan to have one of these trees at Wirksworth?"

Peter raised a brow. "Perhaps I shall. If for no other reason than to prove to you of its existence." He scratched at his cheek. "Would you help me decorate it if I were to cut one down?"

Caroline's eyes widened. The activity would surely mean more time with Peter. "Of course. I know you are in great need of help."

Peter pointed to a tree up ahead. It was smaller than most of the trees around it, only slightly taller than Peter. It had full branches going all the way to the ground, but they tapered in length as they neared the top. The tree was almost a perfect conical shape.

Peter quickened his pace, pulling her along behind him. "This will be the perfect Tannenbaum." He stopped in front of it and looked it up and down. "Yes, this one is perfect, indeed." He turned to her, his eyes glowing with excitement. "Have you ever seen a more perfect tree?"

Caroline raised her shoulders. "I do not know what a perfect tree looks like as I have never before seen one."

Peter's brow furrowed. "You have never seen *what*?"

Caroline squinted at him. "A perfect tree."

His face clouded over and became pensive.

Samuel and Lydia stopped beside them, and her brother sized up the tree. He started to laugh. "What are you thinking, Rockwell? This log shall not last a day, let alone until Epiphany."

Peter gave Samuel a bland look. "It is not for my yule log, you dolt. This one is for a Christmas tree."

"A Christmas tree? What, pray tell, is a Christmas tree?"

Caroline shot her brother a look of annoyance. Why did he and Lydia have to come along? "It is a tree you take indoors and decorate." She stared at him as if he were a complete nodcock, even though she had only learned of what they were moments before.

Samuel shrugged. "It sounds ridiculous. Is there not enough greenery already?"

Caroline gave her foot a little stomp. How dare he call Peter ridiculous. "I'll have you know Princess Caroline puts one up in the royal palace every year. Are you claiming to be better than the princess?"

Samuel muttered something under his breath, but Caroline turned away from him.

Peter stood at the tree. "Will someone help me cut this down?" He looked at Caroline and then Samuel.

Caroline stepped forward. "I will help you."

Samuel pushed her back to her spot by Lydia. "No, you will not. Sawing a tree is not a task for a lady." He grasped hold of the saw handle. "I will help, Rockwell."

The two had the tree down with little more than four pulls on the saw. The footmen rushed forward and grabbed the small tree.

"Please, do not strip those branches. I want that tree to stay intact."

The footman nodded and picked it up, pushing the tree up onto his shoulder and carrying it away. He left the other servants to wait for the next one.

The group wandered around before they spotted the perfect tree for Peter's yule log. He wasted no time in bringing the evergreen to the ground.

"Why do we not go back to the sled and we can warm up while we travel to the holly trees? There is no need for us to walk all that way in the snow." Peter looked to each person for their approval.

Lydia nodded her head as she stomped her feet. "I can scarce feel my toes. I am in favor of your plan, Lord Rockwell."

Samuel held his arm out to his wife and led her back in the direction they had come, leaving Peter and Caroline to take up the rear.

"Why did your mother make such a point of telling you to dress warm?"

Caroline watched her feet as they walked. "It is nothing. She treats me as a child most of the time."

Peter scrunched up his brow. "But she implied you had gone to town yesterday without proper attire. I can attest you had on a very warm cloak and muff. Why should she assume you had not?"

Caroline did not know why she was resistant to tell him what she had done. She knew her mother would never understand her giving the cloak away to a woman in need, but surely Peter would understand. Would he not?

"There was a woman in the village. She was close to her days of confinement and had a little one with her. They looked so cold. I could not turn my back on them. I knew I had a warm home to return to when I was done in the village. I doubted she had such luxuries." She shrugged. "When I returned home, my mother spotted me upon my entry into the house. She saw I was without any kind of warm clothing." Caroline sighed. "She rang such a peal over my head."

Peter stopped in his tracks. "You gave a stranger your cloak and muff?"

Caroline swallowed. He didn't understand either. She had been certain he would. A dull ache formed in her chest.

He shook his head. "You have grown into an amazing woman, Lady Caroline."

The ache was replaced by a flutter. He did understand. "Thank you," was the only thing she could manage to say.

They walked the rest of the way to the sled in silence.

He helped her up into the driver's seat and settled in next to her. Setting the horses into motion, he guided them toward the far end of the forest. It only took a few minutes to get to the holly tree grove.

"Already? I hoped the ride would be longer. My feet are still nearly frozen," Lydia whined from the bench behind.

Caroline looked over her shoulder and saw Samuel pat his wife on the knee. "Why do you not stay here beneath the rug and warm your feet on the bricks?" He looked to Peter. "Caroline, will you stay with Lydia? I am confident Peter and I can fetch plenty of holly and even find some mistletoe, as well."

Caroline's stomach burned. Why must Lydia be so...gah. "Of course, I can stay with dear Lydia." Caroline smiled falsely at her sister-in-law.

Samuel gave her a satisfied smile, to which Caroline scowled. He may have won this battle, but she vowed he would not win the next one.

Peter handed Caroline out of the driver's seat and then helped her back into the sled so she could settle in beside Lydia.

What had started out as such a lovely outing had suddenly turned quite sour.

Caroline pulled the rug over her lap and leaned forward, resting her elbows on her knees. She dropped her head into her hands and sighed.

"He is a handsome man, is he not?" Lydia's voice was quiet beside her.

"Hmmm?" Caroline stared ahead at Peter's retreating back. Lydia's words replayed in her mind and Caroline sat up straight. "Who is quite handsome?"

Lydia smiled and tilted her head to the side, her eyes widening slightly. "As if you do not know my meaning."

Caroline put her hand on her hot cheek. Blast her telling blush. She glanced at Lydia, hoping her sister-in-law would believe it was the cold which caused the pinking.

"Lord Rockwell?" Caroline leaned forward again. If Lydia could not see her face, she could hide her feelings easier. "I suppose he is tolerable."

Lydia chuckled quietly. "I believe you think him more than tolerable."

"He is an old friend, nothing more."

Lydia clucked her tongue. "Samuel believed you to have had a tendré for Lord Rockwell when you were a girl."

Caroline forced a laugh. "Perhaps a very small tendré. But that was nearly ten years past. I believe I have long since moved beyond those feelings." Was Lydia believing any of this? Even with her own ears, Caroline thought she could hear the lie.

"A girl could do worse than a handsome earl. Now that he is back, I cannot suppose he will remain unmarried for long. He is sure to be one of the most sought-after gentlemen of the Season."

The burning in Caroline's stomach. That was precisely what she feared.

𝕾 8 𝕾

"I would be honored if you would join me for tea." Peter addressed them all, but his eyes lingered a little longer on Caroline.

Lady Montjoy pouted slightly. "We should love to join you, but I am afraid Lady Killingsworth expects my immediate return. She is desirous for the decorating to begin as quickly as possible."

Peter frowned at the reins in his hands. If Lady Montjoy was needed, surely Caroline would be also. He flicked the reins harder than was necessary, setting the horses in motion.

The return trip felt quick and only served to darken Peter's mood. Why he felt so out of sorts, he was not entirely certain. He could only owe it to the notion that they were having a delightful time and it was about to come to an end. Had he not felt similar when he was a child and was forced to return home for supper?

He pulled the sled into the courtyard of Whitley Wood. Samuel hopped down immediately and handed out his wife.

Peter moved slower. He wished they'd had more time alone—

more time to talk without Montjoy and his wife constantly within ear shot. But he'd understood the unlikelihood of that happening.

He finally stepped down and handed Caroline out, not wishing for her to catch a chill. He held his arm out to her, leading her to the steps of the castle. Her reserve seemed to slip around her as they moved closer to the entrance.

The footmen scurried about, unloading the greenery that would be staying at Whitley.

"Thank you for accompanying me, Caroline."

She smiled, but it barely turned the tips of her mouth. "It was my pleasure, Lord Rockwell."

Peter scowled. He hated hearing her use his formal title. Were they not past such formalities? Had they ever really observed them before?

Stanton opened the front door for Montjoy, and they all followed in behind him.

Montjoy removed his greatcoat and gloves, handing them off to the butler.

"Oh, good. You have returned." Lady Killingsworth descended the staircase with an air of superiority. Some may call it grace, but Peter knew better. Grace was something his mother had possessed; what Lady Killingsworth had was haughtiness and pride.

"Lady Montjoy, we can begin the decorating as soon as you have warmed yourself. Tea is waiting in the Green Room. Please, do make haste. Evening will wait for no one."

Caroline removed her gloves. "I shall be along shortly, my lady. I am not in need of warming. Lord Rockwell was so kind as to provide plenty of bricks and rugs."

Lady Killingsworth waved her words aside. "You are not needed for this, Caroline. Lady Montjoy is to be mistress, not you."

Caroline's countenance fell and Peter's hands clenched at his side.

He stepped forward. "If you are not in need of her, my lady, I could use her expertise in decorating. Wirksworth is currently without a mistress."

Lady Killingsworth shrugged. "If she could be of use to you, take her."

Caroline's mouth dropped open, before she snapped it shut, her jaw working. She took a step forward. "I shall call for Barton."

Lady Killingsworth waved her away. "Barton is needed here. You go along and enlist the assistance of one of Lord Rockwell's maids."

Caroline's eyes widened. "But Mama. It would not be proper for me to accompany Lord Rockwell without a chaperone."

A smile played at the corners of Peter's mouth. Might he actually get his wish after all?

Lady Killingsworth swished by her daughter, pausing only long enough to toss over her shoulder, "Come now, Caroline. It is Lord Rockwell. He is an old friend. There is nothing scandalous there."

Peter's brows rose slowly into his hairline. Obviously, Lady Killingsworth was not adept at interpreting people. If she knew of Peter's desire to spend time alone with Caroline, the lady might not be so eager to send her off with him alone.

He stepped up beside her. "I do not know your feelings, but I am thrilled by the notion."

Caroline licked her lips, but her eyes stayed focused on the doorway her mother had just passed through. "I am at least happy to be of service to someone."

She did not sound as excited about the prospect of being with him as he was to be with her.

She waited a moment for Stanton to bring back her pelisse and bonnet.

Peter watched as her delicate fingers tied the bow at her chin and then began to worm their way inside her gloves. Had she always been this graceful and refined?

Peter shook his head. No, she had been rough and tumble not so long ago. He gave his head a light shake. That was not entirely right. She may have climbed trees and fished in the stream alongside he and Montjoy, but there had always been a grace about her, even at a young age. Peter had just not paid it any mind before.

Once she was ready again for the weather, Peter held out his arm and escorted her out to his waiting sled.

He knew he should hand her up into the rear seat, but he so badly wished her to sit next to him again. However, he needed to show restraint and be the gentleman his mother had raised him to be.

He moved to hand her up into the rear of the sled and Caroline's brow creased.

"What is wrong, Caroline?"

She bit her lip. "Do you not wish me to ride in the front with you?"

Peter grinned. "Very much so, but I did not believe a gentleman would do such a thing."

Caroline grinned as he handed her up into the sled. "You are not a gentleman. You are Peter, my old childhood friend."

Peter grimaced and settled in beside her. "That was not the response I had hoped for." But at least she was smiling. For now, he would take that over her good opinion.

She moved a little closer to him. "The bricks are no longer warm."

He reached around her and pulled her to him. "Then sit closer. I shall keep you warm until we arrive at Wirksworth." Peter waited for her to pull away, but she did not. His pulse jumped erratically before settling into a quick, pounding rhythm.

He set the horses going, but at a much slower pace than he had before. He did not want to hurry anything about this ride back to Wirksworth.

"Did you really need my help, or were you only feeling sorry for me?"

Peter barely heard her words before they flew past on the wind.

"I am in great need of your help. Why should you think otherwise?"

"You employ plenty of servants. They could easily accomplish the task of decorating Wirksworth for the holidays." She leaned her head against his shoulder and pulled the rug up, holding it just under her chin.

"What did I say that was not true? Wirksworth is, indeed, without a mistress. You cannot think it would be the same to have the servants do all the decorating. Besides, it was one of my favorite things about the holidays." He tilted his head slightly, so it rested on her bonneted head. She fit so perfectly next to him; it was hard not to imagine this was his everyday life. "I used to help my mother every year."

Before he wished it, Wirksworth came into view. At least this was only the beginning of his time with her and not the end.

James jogged from the stables as they pulled into the yard.

Caroline sat up, putting more distance between them. The cold was instantly noticeable.

Peter hopped out and held out his hand to her.

"Has the other sled already returned, James?"

The old man nodded. "Yes, my lord. They have taken the log and the greenery inside."

Peter clapped the man lightly on the back. "Good, good. Rub

them down and give them a good feeding. They have earned it."
He ran his hand down the side of the nearest horse.

"Will do, my lord."

James led the horses and the sled away and Peter led Caroline
to the front door.

"I have not been here in an age." She paused and looked up at
the front of the large house.

"Has it changed much from what you remember?"

Porter opened the door wide until Peter and Caroline had
both crossed the threshold.

Caroline turned in a small circle, looking around her. "It looks
so much smaller than I remember."

Peter chuckled. "Excuse me?"

She turned toward him, her brow creased. "I only meant that
the perspective of a young girl is much different than my current
one."

Peter nudged her with his shoulder. "I know what you meant.
I was only having a little fun with you."

Caroline grinned. "You are a wicked man, Lord Rockwell. I
thought, perhaps I had offended you."

"You could never offend me, Caroline."

Her face flushed. Did she welcome such comments from him?

"Come. Let us begin with the greenery about the entryway
and staircase. Then we shall finish up with the Tannenbaum."

A pile of evergreen boughs lay on a cloth spread out at the side
of the staircase. Several spools of ribbon were stacked in a pile next
to them.

Peter put his hand on the small of her back. A tingling vibrated
up his hand and into his arm. Surprised, he pulled it away.

She looked at him over her shoulder.

He smiled and motioned her toward the evergreen boughs.

Picking up a branch, he twirled it around in his fingers. He looked at it curiously, realizing how little he had actually done when helping his mother decorate.

He glanced over at Caroline, hoping she had some notion of what to do with all these branches. She picked several up and bundled them together, twisting one branch this way and another that way. She tilted her head and squinted. Moving a different branch, she smiled and finally looked up at him. "Could you fetch me the ribbon? I need to tie this off."

Peter stooped down and reached for a spool. Placing his hand on his thigh, he pushed himself to standing.

He extended the ribbon to her. "Could you please wrap the ribbon at this spot between my hands?"

Peter pulled several hands of ribbon from the spool and snipped it off with the shears, returning the rest of the ribbon to the nearby table. He wrapped the ribbon around the bundle and tied it in a knot. The ribbon hung limply down the sides.

Peter stared at it. This was not what he remembered it looking like when his mother had done it. He glanced up at Caroline.

She grinned and placed the bundle in his hands. Taking a step closer to him, she looped the ribbon around her finger, her head bent low.

Peter stared at the gentle slope of her neck where it curved into her shoulder. The scent of lilacs drifted up to his nose.

He leaned slightly over her, closing his eyes and letting the scent envelope him.

The bundle shifted in his hands.

"What do you think of the bow, Peter?"

He opened his eyes but did not move until her head came up and connected with his chin. His teeth slammed together, and his entire mouth hurt.

"Ooph." Caroline straightened, rubbing at the crown of her

head. "I am sorry, Peter. I did not realize you were leaning over to watch."

Peter squeezed his eyes shut, pushing the tears that burned behind his lids back. It would only make her feel worse and for something that was entirely his fault.

He reached out and gently stroked her hair. "It is I who should apologize. I was the nodcock leaning over you. How were you to know?"

She seemed to lean into his hand, and he took a step closer.

"Are you well? We can take a break and have some tea." His chest tightened and he wanted to pull her closer. What was happening? This was little Lady Caroline. He took a step back, putting a safe distance between them.

She shook her head. "We have only just started. If we stop now, we shall never finish on time." She frowned. "Lady Killingsworth would not approve if we are late for supper."

Peter sighed when she dropped down to the floor and kneeled beside the cloth. She straightened her skirts, covering the whole of her feet and looked up at him. "Come. If we are both working on them, we shall finish this task quicker."

Peter smirked at her but dropped down onto the floor next to her. This was the relationship he knew and was comfortable with.

Caroline gathered several more branches. "Do you want to hold or tie the bows?"

Peter snorted. "After my last attempt, I think it best if I hold while you tie." He rubbed at his jaw. "I shall keep my chin away from your head this time. I promise."

Caroline reached a hand up, running her thumb along his jaw. "Oh, it is all red. I did not realize I hit you so hard." She glanced up and met his gaze. "Does it hurt very badly?"

Peter shook his head almost imperceptibly. "Not anymore." His voice was quiet.

"I am glad to hear it." She pulled her hand away and Peter felt himself leaning forward after it. He jerked back. What was he doing? She was going to think him the most wanton rake she had ever met.

"We are not making much progress." She shoved the branches into his hand and quickly tied a bow.

Without looking at him again, she continued to bundle branches and push them into his hands, moving the process along at a much faster pace.

They moved to the staircase tying the greenery up the railing. Once they finished, Peter stepped back to look at the finished product.

"It is lovely and just as I remember from my when my mother decorated."

Caroline frowned. "Something is missing." She moved over to the cloth on the floor and moved the remaining pine boughs. "It is no wonder the bunches look so plain. We forgot the holly."

She cut off a dozen stems of the waxy green leaves. Stopping at every bunch along the way, she worked the holly, with its red berries peeking out, into the bundles.

They stepped back once more. Peter smiled. "You are right. The holly adds more depth and color. *This* is what I remember."

Caroline smiled, but her eyes remained on the greenery.

Peter pulled out his pocket watch and glanced down the corridor. "We have just enough time to decorate the Tannenbaum before I must return you home."

They entered a small parlor on the back side of the house.

"I do not remember this room. Did we never come in it as children?"

Peter sighed deeply. "It was my mother's parlor. She came in here for quiet and solitude."

Caroline chuckled. "That is something we certainly did not provide."

He moved to the corner and pulled the cord. Turning back to the center of the room, he asked, "Where do you think is the best spot for the tree?"

Caroline walked to the bay window overlooking the rear gardens. "I think this is the perfect spot. What do you think?"

Peter came up behind her; looking out over the estate, he could just make out the outline of Whitley Wood—a new reason to like this room. "I believe you are right."

A young maid entered and curtsied. "My lord."

Peter turned toward her. "Clara, is it not?"

The girl nodded, a slight pink tinging her cheeks.

"Clara, would you please ask Walter and Carter to bring the tree in here? I also need the basket of cranberries from the kitchen and some needles threaded with fishing twine."

The girl looked at him oddly but nodded and moved from the room.

Peter walked to the small writing desk at the far side. He pulled several boxes from the top side drawer and brought them over, handing one to Caroline. She opened the box and peered inside. "Oh, the candles."

He nodded and handed her the second box. "Please excuse me for a moment. I need to retrieve something from my chambers." He turned to quit the room but paused and turned back. "Promise me you will not leave. I will return shortly."

Why had he felt it necessary to make her promise? Did he think she might flee as soon as his back was turned or was it that he was so completely enjoying himself, he did not wish her to misinterpret his departure? Whatever the reason, he was quite sure he sounded completely bacon brained.

She smiled and nodded as he walked out of the room.

Peter quickened his pace and took the stairs two at a time, jogging down the corridor and into his chambers.

He knelt in front of his trunk, and yanked open the lid, rummaging around inside for the object of his search.

His hand grazed over the top of a pasteboard box and he thrust both hands in to withdraw it. He opened the box and lifted out a small brass candle holder with a curved clip on the underside.

Dropping the holder back into the box, Peter slammed the top shut on the chest and hurried from the room.

By the time he reached the parlor, the Tannenbaum was already situated in front of the window. Peter stopped in the doorway, his breath catching in his throat.

Caroline stood on her tiptoes, silhouetted against the window, reaching up into the branches of the tree.

She glanced over and saw him standing in the doorway. She dropped down onto flat feet and took several steps toward him. "It is beautiful just as it is, do you not agree?"

Peter swallowed hard. "Yes, it is." His chest felt tight. His eyes never left her face. It was a beautiful scene and he was disappointed to think it would come to an end. For the first time, he wondered if it *did* need to end. What if he could have her here with him forever? His brow furrowed. Was he merely enchanted by the scene? Or did he truly wish to form an attachment with Caroline?

He held the pasteboard box out in front of him. "I have the candle holders." His voice came out flat and lifeless. This new realization about Caroline made him feel unsure and awkward.

She seemed not to notice. "Do we affix the candles first?" She took the box from his hands and opened the lid, lifting one out. Walking to the writing desk, she set the box down and picked up a candle lying there, placing it in the little cup.

Peter moved up behind her. He took the candle from her and

their fingers brushed. He felt her breath hitch, which caused his to do the same. Lady Killingsworth was quite mistaken in her belief that there was no danger from Peter. He felt rather dangerous just then.

He took a step back. "We need to string the cranberries first and drape them on the tree. Then we can add the candles." He led her over to the settee and picked up the basket of red fruit, setting it between them. He hoped the distance would allow him to clear his mind. Taking the needle, he pushed a berry onto it and threaded it down to the knot at the end of the twine.

"Did you learn this in Westphalia also?"

Peter nodded. "Yes. Herr Schöenbacher was very kind to include me in his family's celebrations."

Caroline concentrated on the cranberry in her hand. "What did you study while you lived there?"

"Music." Peter watched his needle, but his glance kept drifting over to Caroline. He poked his finger. "Ouch." A drop of blood formed, and he stuck it in his mouth.

"As a survivor of years of needlework treachery, I'd advise you to pay more heed to the location of your needle." Caroline followed her own advice, keeping her eyes focused on the needle in front of her. But a smile played at her lips.

"Your warning is too late, Caroline. I have already drawn blood." His words were slightly slurred around the finger in his mouth.

She laughed. "I believe you are only trying to get out of working. But I shall not let you out of the task."

Peter lifted the needle back up and pushed a cranberry onto the point, making sure to keep his fingers to the sides of the fruit. "It will be worth the work. I promise you that."

They both went quiet as they concentrated on their work. Peter worked hard to keep his focus off the woman beside him, but was not wholly successful, poking himself several more times.

"Perhaps this will give you a better appreciation of the perils we ladies face in our daily stitching routine."

Peter stared at her. There had been a moment back in the forest when he thought she had sounded familiar. Not Caroline familiar, but Miss Tree familiar. This conversation felt like one he would have with the mystery lady. Could it be possible or was he simply imagining it because he wished it to be true?

A tingle started in Peter's stomach. He sighed exaggeratedly. "I had no notion you were taking your life into your hands each time you sat with the basket at your side. Why would you take such risks?"

She grinned. "It is what is required of a lady, my lord. No eligible gentleman would take a second glance at a woman unable to complete an elegant sampler. It is one of the burdens society has cast upon us." She glanced up, pausing in her threading. "Tell me, my lord. Would you ever consider a woman without such attributes to her credit?"

Peter cocked a brow. "Now that I know the peril you face, I shall forbid any lady in my home from taking such a risk."

Caroline laughed loudly and he thought he might burst at the sound. What could he say that would cause such a reaction again? Now that he had heard it, he needed to hear it over and over again.

He looked in front of them and saw the long strings of cranberries. Gently carrying them, he took them over to the tree. Lifting his arms, he draped the berries on the branches. Caroline stood back and told him where to put each one so the drape was consistent.

She ran to the entryway and retrieved the ribbon, tying bows to add to some of the branches.

Together, they added the candles. Once they were all on the

tree, Peter called for Walter and Carter to help him light them. The sun had just dropped below the horizon, leaving the grounds outside the window in almost darkness.

Over a hundred tiny flickers of light lit the room. Caroline clapped her hands together and whispered. "Oh, Peter. It is the most beautiful thing I have ever seen."

He moved in behind her and sighed. "We did well, Caroline. Herr Schöenbacher had nothing so lovely."

They both stood there in silence, the candlelight flickering in their eyes. A part of him wanted to reach around her and pull her back against him, but he did not. Instead he clasped his hands behind his back to ensure he did not make a grave mistake. But would embracing Caroline be a mistake?

He gave a slight shake of his head. Until he knew for certain the answer to that question, he must keep himself in check where Lady Caroline was concerned.

9

Caroline grimaced at her reflection, turning her head one way and then the other. "Barton, is there something more you could do with my hair?" Her stomach flopped.

Peter was to join them for the evening and after the time they had spent together that afternoon, she felt both frazzled and excited.

Barton nodded. "Of course, my lady." She took the pins out of Caroline's hair, letting the hair fall down her back.

Caroline let out a small gasp. "I did not intend for you to start over, Barton."

The girl shrugged. "It is no trouble." She pulled two strings of pearls, each pearl spaced a finger width apart, from a drawer in the jewelry box. Pulling the sides of Caroline's hair back, she weaved the pearl strands into plaits at the side and into the knot at the back of her head.

Barton stood back. "Is this to your liking, my lady?"

Small plaits drooped daintily before curving around the knot, forming a sort of tiara at the crown of her head.

Caroline tilted her head to the side. Would Peter like it? She did not know if he had a preference toward pearls. "Very much, Barton. Thank you for taking the extra time, tonight. I wanted something special for Christmas Eve."

Caroline glanced at Barton to see if the girl recognized the lie.

Barton had turned away to pick up a pin which had fallen to the floor. "Yes, I can imagine you would, my lady."

Pushing back from the table, Caroline moved to the dressing screen and allowed Barton to help lift the gown over her head.

Red silk fell around her body, cooling her heated skin. Barton tied the silver ribbon at Caroline's back.

"Would you like to wear your pearl pendant, my lady?"

Caroline nodded. "Yes, I think I would."

Barton fastened the necklace and Caroline turned back to the mirror. She turned her head from one side to the other, checking all aspects of her gown and hair.

Everything Barton had done should make Caroline feel beautiful. But she did not. Pretty, perhaps, but not beautiful. She felt like the same old Caroline. How would she ever convince Peter she was not the same little girl she had been when he left if she could not even make herself appealing to him?

She turned away from the mirror. It was not making her any more handsome standing there looking. So why torture herself any longer?

The clock struck seven, causing both relief and panic to course through her. Even now, Peter was likely in the parlor.

She swallowed hard and squared her shoulders, not wanting to give her mother anything more to criticize her for tonight.

She walked down the corridor feeling completely undesirable

and knew it would only worsen when her mother caught sight of her.

As she neared the top of the stairs, panic overtook the excitement. She paused with her hand on the railing. Perhaps she should forgo supper and take a tray in her room. Her heart felt fragile tonight.

Standing in front of Peter's Tannenbaum, with all the candles lit, as the sun dropped below the horizon, had stirred feelings she had been trying unsuccessfully to put aside. While the tree had been lovely, it was his nearness that had captured her awareness. She had almost felt his hand rest at the small of her back, but it had never happened. Why should it? He still did not see her as a woman, the way he constantly joked and made light of things. And Samuel had told her Peter had brought a lady from France to marry. Why could Caroline not let go?

The longer she stood rooted in place, the greater her desire to return to her room. Someone cleared their throat and it echoed up the stairway.

Caroline looked for the source. Peter stood at the bottom, looking altogether too handsome in his black tailcoat with the small peek of silver from his waistcoat. All her earlier thoughts of skipping supper fled and she felt herself being pulled down the stairs toward him. Even with the inevitable criticism Mama was sure to throw at her, being in the same room with Peter would be worth it.

He waited until she stepped off the last stair before presenting her his arm. "Caroline, you are a vision tonight."

Could he be sincere or was it merely politeness?

"Thank you, my lord." She fell back on formality to help hide the tremble she felt traveling up her legs and into her stomach.

She entered the drawing room on his arm.

Mama looked up from her conversation with Lydia.

"Thank you for joining us, Caroline. Perhaps you forgot we are keeping country hours, not town hours."

Caroline swallowed. "I apologize, my lady. There were complications with my hair."

Lady Killingsworth nodded. "Yes, I can see that." She tsked. "If you were not so late already, I might suggest you return and have Barton fix it. But we do not have time for all that."

Peter stiffened at her side. "I think her hair lovely. I saw nothing its equal, even in London."

Her mother shrugged and returned to her conversation with Lydia.

Caroline looked up at him, but he was staring at her mother, his face set in a stony mask.

Stanton announced dinner and everyone paired up to proceed into the dining room. Caroline placed her hand on Peter's arm.

At the doorway, Lord Killingsworth stepped into the corridor and paused. Samuel and Lydia stepped through the threshold and Lord Killingsworth stopped them. "Ha, my son. You are caught under the kissing ball." He chuckled at his own joke.

Samuel grinned good naturally at his father and leaned forward and placed a quick kiss on his wife's lips. Lydia blushed as they hurried out from under the mistletoe.

Caroline glanced up at Peter and then at her father. Surely the kissing ball was only for the benefit of the married couples and her father would allow Peter and her to pass through. While she had never wanted anything more than to have Peter kiss her, she wanted him to do so because he desired it, not because he felt compelled to kiss her. The possibility that he might object was more than she could take. It would be better to not even be presented with the option.

She glanced at her mother. *Please, for once, use propriety to help me.*

When she looked back at Peter, he winked at her.

What did he mean by that? Did he hope her father stopped them? Her heart thumped in her chest and her hands began to shake the nearer they came to the threshold. She tightened her hand on Peter's arm to stop the quiver.

Peter led her through the doorway, and just as she hoped and feared, her father put out his hand and stopped Peter under the kissing ball. "Come, Rockwell. You are under the kissing ball. I'm sure Caroline would oblige you a kiss."

Caroline dropped her hands to her side, her fists clenching. She bit her bottom lip, watching through lowered lashes as Peter leaned toward her. She expected him to waggle his eyebrows or grin at her as he kissed her, treat it as the joke he surely thought that it was.

But he did not. His gaze caught hold of hers and held it as he came closer.

Caroline could not be sure she was remembering to breathe. But she must have because she still stood waiting for his lips to come down on hers.

He stopped only a breath away from her lips and Caroline's eyes fluttered closed. She waited but nothing happened.

"Caroline, you may open your eyes now. Lord Rockwell is not interested in kissing you."

The sound of Lady Killingsworth's voice washed over her like pond water in early March. Caroline opened her eyes, searching for Peter. He stood with his back against the door frame, his face telling her he wished himself far away from here.

"Nonsense, Lady Killingsworth. I should be honored to kiss your daughter." He reached forward and placed a kiss on the back of Caroline's hand.

Caroline's breath wedged beneath the knot in her throat. Oh, could this moment get any worse?

Heat filled her face and the sound of blood filled her ears, drowning out any other noise in the room.

Lord Rockwell does not wish to kiss you. The words repeated over and over in her brain, until she could barely continue standing upright. Why had she not taken a tray in her room?

Her throat tightened until she did not think she could stand it a moment longer. Tears were imminent.

But Mama would not stand for such improper behavior. Caroline stepped from the doorway and into the hall. She needed to compose herself and quickly. If she cried off now, everyone would know she was in love with Peter and she could not handle the lecture which would follow.

Caroline sucked her breath in through her teeth, willing her pulse to slow down. Perhaps if she thought on something calming and relaxing, she might be able to ward off the tears that threatened. What was calming? Sheep? They were soft and at times cuddly. Their soft bleating had often left her feeling relaxed. Her heart slowed. If she could just keep her thoughts on sheep, she may just be able to keep control through dinner. Then she could plead a headache and retire before the rest of the evening's festivities.

CAROLINE LOOKED up at her ceiling. How had she allowed herself to be in this situation? The utter humiliation of the evening flooded over her anew. She finally allowed a tear to drop free. It ran down the side of her face, wetting the hair at her temple.

She recounted each moment, trying to decide what choice she could have made to achieve a different result. The conclusion was that she should have taken a tray in her room and not allowed the other choices to ever present themselves.

The sound of the pianoforte and voices drifted up to her chambers. She could hear her mother's perfectly tuned alto and Samuel's tenor voices blend together. A less pleasant soprano seemed incongruent with the other voices. Lydia. Caroline almost felt sorry she was not downstairs to help her sister-in-law with the soprano part, but not bad enough to abandon her bed.

A rich, warm bass joined in and Caroline felt as if a knife stabbed into her chest. She had nearly forgotten Peter could sing. It seemed his time with Herr Schöenbacher had improved upon something that had already been very pleasant.

Caroline rolled to her side and pulled a pillow over her head, squishing it down hard against her ear with her arm.

She squeezed her eyes shut and muted her ears. If she focused hard enough, she was able to fill them with something like the sound of waves breaking against the rocks. Or, that is what she imagined waves would sound like. She had never actually heard the sound for herself. Perhaps she would think about removing herself to the Cornish coast or the coast of Scotland when the holidays were over. Surely Mama would not object, not if it meant being rid of Caroline and the constant reminder of her marital failures.

It really did not matter where she went, as long as she was anywhere Peter was not.

❦ 10 ❦

Peter paced in front of the Tannenbaum. How had an evening with such promise ended so utterly poorly?

Why had he glanced at Samuel? And why had Samuel shaken his head and scowled at him?

Peter had endured the rest of the evening even after Caroline had cried off, but only out of politeness.

And maybe because he had secretly hoped she might come back down when they started to sing Christmas carols. But she had not. Now he was left with guilt and confusion about his feelings for her. Indeed, he had even begun to question how he felt about Miss Tree.

When he had left London, he was determined to return after the holidays and discover the identity of the mystery woman. But over the last few days, those desires had waned. He still wished to know who she was, but the matter felt far less pressing than it had a week ago.

Peter stood as Jennings brushed down his coat.

A knock sounded and Porter pushed open the door. "Merry

Christmas, my lord. A letter has arrived for you." He walked over to Peter and handed him the folded paper.

Peter turned it over in his hands, immediately recognizing the seal of Montjoy pressed into the wax. "Thank you, Porter."

The butler slipped from the room.

Jennings gave one last firm brush and bent to retrieve a shirt from off the floor. "Do you wish to take a tray here or will you be going down to the breakfast room, my lord?"

Peter waved him away. "I will be down shortly. You may go, Jennings. Thank you."

The valet slipped through the dressing room door and out of sight.

Peter cracked the seal on the note and opened it up.

Care for a match with swords before the Christmas festivities begin? Meet me in the Hall of the Guard at 11.

Montjoy

Peter straightened his coat and checked his reflection one last time. Swords seemed an appropriate idea this morning. Perhaps he could take a little of his frustrations out on Montjoy. Afterall, he had been the cause of this whole mess.

PETER PULLED his arms from his tailcoat and folded it in half down the back. He draped it over the back of a nearby chair. Loosening the buttons on his waistcoat, he tossed it to the chair also. "Thank you for suggesting a bout. I have not used blades in an age." Peter selected his words carefully.

Montjoy grinned as he loosened his cravat. "I will try to take it easy on you. At least in the beginning."

The man did not even know he had done anything wrong. It

was as if he had not even been at supper last night. Only he had and he'd made a complete muddle of it.

Peter dropped his head from side to side, rotating his shoulders to rid himself of any tightness.

Perhaps he should not place the entirety of the blame on Montjoy. Afterall, Peter was the one who had pulled back from the kiss. He could have ignored Montjoy's warning and continued with his original intentions. But he had not and therein was the problem. "It is most kind of you, *my friend.*" The last words came out harder than Peter had intended. He was beginning to question if, indeed, Montjoy was still his friend. "But I do not think it necessary. I am sure I will be back to besting you in no time."

Montjoy laughed loudly. "I see your confidence is just as large as ever."

Peter smiled and shrugged. "One does not let an opponent see your weaknesses. Not that I have a weakness." He picked up the foil and moved it in a tight circle. Placing his hand behind his back, he shuffled his feet back and forth. "You see? It is as if I had never put the blade down at all."

Montjoy moved into place. "We will see about that." He touched the tip of Peter's sword. "En-garde."

Peter bounced lightly on his feet. Lunging forward, he knocked Montjoy's blade away. His muscles loosened and his head began to clear. Why had he not done this sooner?

"You have been spending a great deal of time with Caroline." Montjoy's tone had lost its playfulness.

Peter lunged and Montjoy blocked. "I enjoy her company. Why do I sense you are not happy about it?" He shuffled back, moving out of the way as Montjoy launched with more force than Peter expected. The blade tip poked Peter in the ribs and his brows furrowed. "Ooph. I thought you were taking it easy."

Montjoy smirked. "My apologies. I did not realize I had used so much force." He stepped back, waving his hand in front of him. "I will try to restrain myself—for now." They both reset their positions.

Peter leveled a stare at Montjoy. "What is bothering you? I sense there is something between us, something I did not feel when we were together in London."

Montjoy kept his blade in position. "En-garde." He shuffled toward Peter. "My sister did not know of your return while we were in London."

Peter paused and Montjoy took the advantage poking Peter in the right shoulder. He laughed. "You were wrong, Rockwell. You *have* become slow in your years without practice."

Peter rubbed at his shoulder. "I have not become soft. I was trying to decipher your meaning. You are taking advantage of the conversation." He scowled at Montjoy and moved back into place. "What do you mean Caroline did not know I had returned? Why should that change our relationship and make you angry with me?"

Peter's stomach twisted. This conversation felt as though it could be a breaking point for their friendship. But he needed clarification. He needed to know why Montjoy was so decidedly against Peter spending time with Caroline. Had Montjoy sensed Peter's changing feelings? Did he object to a more intimate association between he and Caroline? The whole thing was rather absurd, considering Peter did not even know his feelings for Caroline.

Montjoy scoffed. "Come now, man. You know she's had a tendré for you since she was a girl. I had thought when you were away for so long that she would have turned her affections elsewhere." Montjoy sighed and smartly moved several steps back from the tip of Peter's blade. "But now that you have returned, I am afraid she may think herself in love with you still." Montjoy looked down at his feet and Peter took the advantage. He lunged forward and stuck Montjoy in the thigh.

Montjoy's eyes widened in surprise, his mouth slightly agape. He chuckled. "Touché, Rockwell."

"Is it so terrible that she should turn her attentions to me? I thought myself rather a good catch." Peter's previously clear mind clouded over. The notion that Montjoy found Peter lacking as a suitor for Caroline stung. Add to that Montjoy's assertions about Caroline's feelings for Peter, and Peter felt like a jumble of emotions. Many of which he did not understand.

Montjoy cleared his throat and motioned them back into starting position. Peter waited for the signal to begin. Perhaps it was best to evaluate his feelings later and focus on this match Montjoy was currently controlling.

"En-garde." They shuffled toward the center, each man keeping their guard up, their swords blocking each attempt to score the point. When they were both paying attention, they were quite evenly matched.

"You need not stand on pretense with me, Rockwell. I understand the life of a gentleman—not tied down by a wife, traveling to exotic places."

Peter squinted at Montjoy, but kept his sword moving. What was he gabbing on about? What was this life he claimed to understand? And what did he mean by it?

"It is quite well known that you have brought a young lady over from France." Montjoy grimaced. "Did you always plan to marry her, or did circumstances arise which forced your hand? Are there others? You have traveled to many places."

Peter dropped the foil to his side. His other hand tightening in and out of a fist. It sounded as if Montjoy was inferring Peter had done something unthinkable with Gabrielle. "Do you believe I have ruined Miss Babineaux? Implying I did something similar in other places I lived over the last ten years?" He walked to the side of the room and dropped his foil onto the chair. He snatched up his waistcoat, not even bothering to put it on. He draped it over his arm. "If you believe that, you never really knew me."

How could Montjoy, the man Peter thought knew him better than anyone in the world, think such a thing? It was no wonder he had given such a menacing look when Peter was to kiss Caroline under the kissing ball.

Montjoy rushed over, putting a hand on Peter's arm to stop him. "I did not intend to offend you. I only meant to tell you I understand. It is just that Caroline will *not* and I think she deserves someone who is not so...worldly."

Peter's eyes widened. "Worldly?" He grabbed his foil case and tossed the blade inside. "For your information, Gabrielle was not yet thirteen years old when I lived in Lyon. I do not ruin young girls, Montjoy. In point of fact, I have never ruined young ladies or even old ladies."

Peter stomped toward the door, his hand clutching so tightly around the handle of the case, his knuckles blanched. He turned back around. "I could understand others in Lords thinking such things about me, but I did not believe it of you." He walked quickly from the room, taking the steps to the entry two at a time.

He did not wait for his greatcoat, or even for the groom to ready his horse, choosing instead, to send a footman for it later. Distance is what he needed. Distance from Montjoy, from Caroline, distance from people in general.

Peter stomped down the path that ran between the two estates. The cold bite in the air felt good against his hot skin. The wind blew. His fingers burned, not from the tightness of his fist, but because in his rush to leave the house, he had not retrieved his gloves. He moved the case into the other hand, tucking his free hand into his axilla. How could Montjoy believe such a notion? He shook his head, stopping mid-shake and halting him in his tracks. Blast it all. Had Montjoy told Caroline of the rumor? Peter ran his fingers up and down between his brows.

A strong wind set his feet in motion once again. Clutching his foil case in his hand, he jogged the rest of the way back to Wirksworth Hall.

He pushed through the front door. "Porter," he hollered in the entryway.

The man came walking quickly down the stairs. "Yes, my lord?" He was slightly winded from his hasty jaunt.

He finally took the time to replace his waistcoat and tailcoat, shoving his arms inside with great force. "I am freezing. Please have tea sent to my study immediately." Peter started for the stairs.

"I thought you were to spend the afternoon at Whitley Wood."

"I changed my mind," Peter snapped. "I will be in my bookroom."

"Yes, my lord."

Peter threw open the door to his bookroom, sending it banging into the wall behind it. He cringed at the mark it surely made in the wood paneling but did not care to examine it just now. A chill ran down his body. He could not wait for a maid. Grabbing the fire iron, he stoked the coals in the andirons.

The door opened and Peter turned around. "You were most timely, thank...."

Porter stood in the doorway, but there was no tea tray in his hands.

"Begging your pardon, my lord. Lord Montjoy is asking to see you."

Peter moved to the chair beside the fire and sat down. "Tell him I am not at home."

"I tried, sir. But he insisted he knew you were here. He said he watched you walk as far as the tree line. He said he would not leave until he has seen you."

Peter grunted. It was just like Montjoy. Had he not offered all the offensive remarks he had planned? Had he come to reiterate his disapproval of Peter and Caroline? Was there even a Peter and Caroline? Not if Montjoy had his way. "Where is he waiting?"

Porter stood stoically by the door. "In the Yellow Parlor, my lord."

Peter rolled his shoulders several times. "Move him to the library, Porter. Make him comfortable; he will be there for some time." He lifted his chin high before offering a crisp nod. He hoped Montjoy understood the slight. "Now, could I please get that tea before I catch my death of a cold?"

Porter nodded. "Yes, my lord. I will have it sent up immediately." He turned and closed the door behind him.

Montjoy was here. Peter did not know what there was left for the man to say to him. Either he had come to cast more accusations, or he was here to offer apologies, neither of which Peter was interested in hearing.

He moved to the chair behind his desk, turning it to face the window. He stared out at the whiteness. While it hurt to think that Montjoy had thought such terrible things, the thought that Caroline might have heard such rumors made his stomach roil and his chest feel as though someone were standing on top of him, pushing down.

Gabrielle seemed to be at the center of all this. He had hoped having her settled with Eleanor would have stopped the gossips, but he had underestimated the English *Ton*.

Somehow his plan to fund the girl's Season had found the ears of the gabsters. Although, why they found it such a delicious piece of news, he had no notion.

Peter sighed. How would these rumors affect her upcoming

Season? Would she be deemed ruined before she was even presented at court? Would he and Eleanor be able to find her a suitable match?

His fingers drummed on the arm of his chair. He was irritated by what people were saying of him, but the thought of Gabrielle being ruined over this—. He scrubbed his palms over his eyes, rubbing hard and fast.

And to complicate matters, Caroline may be aware of it all. Had she already heard the rumors? He hoped not. She had not said she had been in London of late, so perhaps she was not aware of the on dit. Unless, Samuel had shared them with her.

Why did it bother him so, if Caroline did know? Only a few days ago, he would have been concerned over whether or not Miss Tree had learned of the rumors. Tare an' hounds, if he did not find himself far more concerned about Caroline's opinion of him.

A knock sounded and the maid brought in tea. She moved to set it on the low table by the fireplace.

"You may leave the tea, but please bring another cup. I shall be sharing it with Lord Montjoy."

The maid nodded and headed back the way she had come. "Yes, my lord."

Peter rolled his shoulders, trying to relieve the knot in the back of his neck. It did little good.

He stood up and moved to the bell pull in the corner. He pulled the bell and returned to his seat to wait for Porter to come.

"You rang, my lord?" Peter admired how quickly the man came. No one would guess this house had been without a master for so long. The staff had not slacked in all those years. It was commendable and Peter was grateful for such a reliable and loyal staff.

"Please show Lord Montjoy in."

The butler nodded.

Only moments later the maid returned with the extra cup. As she left the room, Porter arrived with Montjoy. "Lord Montjoy, my lord."

Peter stood up and walked toward the door. Montjoy entered and Peter was pleased with the look of guilt and contrition on his face.

"Would you care to join me? You must be chilled after your ride here."

Montjoy stood still. "I have come to apologize."

Peter shrugged. "I assumed as much." He knew he should be more gracious in accepting Montjoy's apology, but the burning in his stomach and tightness of his chest made it difficult to comply with the niceties of society. He moved to the chair next to the fireplace and sat down, Montjoy following behind.

Montjoy looked at him expectantly. "Do you accept it?"

Peter raised a brow. "Accept what? You have done nothing but tell me what your intentions are." He was being difficult and even somewhat childish, but he did not care. Montjoy should be made to apologize outright. It was the least he could do.

The man swallowed. "I am sorry, Peter. I should have been a better friend. I know the kind of man you were before you left, but you were gone for so long. A man can change in that amount of time—many have."

Peter tilted his head to the side and poured the tea. "It seems you have come here to justify your accusations, rather than apologize."

Montjoy grimaced. "You are right. I am sorry—sorry for believing you a scoundrel and for trying to justify my own terrible behavior. I hope you can forgive me, and that we can be the best of friends again."

Peter kept his eyes averted. He wanted to stay mad at Montjoy —it was what the man deserved. But the truth was, Peter *had* been absent for a long time. He did not have many friends to his credit any longer, most having forgotten him while he was away.

And Montjoy was correct. Men did change in ten years. Indeed, Peter had changed from a selfish entitled boy to, he hoped, a responsible and kind man.

Perhaps Montjoy had not been so misguided in questioning Peter's past. Would he not have done the same if it were Eleanor's affections at stake?

He offered a small grin. "I suppose I can forgive you. In truth, I should not have reacted so poorly."

"I am glad for it." Montjoy nodded slowly, but apprehension showed on his face. "There have been no women? None at all?"

Peter frowned. "None. Is that so hard to believe?"

"I understand Miss Babineaux is a beautiful young lady—" Montjoy looked over his teacup as he took a sip.

Peter opened his mouth to protest. "A pretty girl who is not yet sixteen, Montjoy. Her father died and I promised him I would protect her."

"I understand she was only a child when you were there. But surely there were others who were just as pretty and of the right age."

Peter pushed up taller in his seat, his breath coming out in a controlled huff. "There were *no* other women, Montjoy."

"Then I am satisfied." He must have sensed Peter's simmering irritation and decided to end the conversation. Reaching for a small sandwich from the tray, he took a bite, offering Peter a smile as he chewed.

Peter took a tea cake from the plate. Montjoy had not been wrong. There had been many women he could have chosen. But there was not one who seemed right; who seemed to fit with the picture he had in his mind when he thought of a wife. And he was not one to trifle with a lady if he had no intentions of marrying her.

Peter was tired of this argument. "Is Caroline to accompany you and Lady Montjoy to London after the holiday?" He grimaced internally at the obvious direction he had turned the conversation.

Montjoy helped himself to a cake and took a large bite. He shook his head. "She will return to London, but not with us. She will still be a chaperone for my cousin, as she was before the holidays." Montjoy looked to the ceiling. "It is quite an undertaking. The girl is determined to ruin herself and her family. I understand Caroline had to intervene and save her from complete ruination at a ball just the night before she was set to return home to Whitley."

Peter's brow furrowed. "She was in London before the holiday?"

Montjoy nodded. "And none too happy about it, either. It was my mother's idea. She believes if Caroline refuses to marry, then she should at least be of use to those needing chaperones."

There were many questions the conversation brought to mind, but Peter grasped onto the most recent one first. "What do you mean she refuses to marry?"

Montjoy grinned. "She has turned down three offers. I believe it is because she could never find a gentleman who measured up to you, in her mind."

Peter sputtered on the tea he swallowed. "What? Why should you say such a thing?"

Montjoy tilted his head, his mouth slightly agape. "You can be a dolt at times, Rockwell. I already told you Caroline thought herself in love with you."

Peter shrugged, even as his pulse pounded in his neck. "But she was only a child then. Surely she grew out of it."

"I had thought it so until you arrived here." Montjoy raised a brow. "Now I am less certain."

❧ 11 ❧

Peter moved down the corridor. He had slept very ill and his mind was still in turmoil. If Montjoy was to be believed, Caroline was in love with him.

He had spent most of the night thinking on all of their past conversations, trying to judge the truthfulness of the assertion. Peter could not see it.

In all their interactions, he had thought her friendly—the kind of friendliness naturally born of knowing someone the whole of their lives. Was he missing something? In other encounters he had known when a lady was interested. He shrugged. But Caroline was not like other ladies.

Her feelings were not the only questions swirling around in his mind. She had been in London before coming to Warwickshire. And what of this ball she had attended on the eve of her departure from London. Was it Lord Trenton's ball or another? Peter had been invited to no less than four other balls occurring on that very night. It was possible she had attended one of those.

But had not Miss Tree left him on the dance floor in order to save her cousin from making a mistake? Was it the kind of mistake which would cause her ruin or something else? If Caroline were Miss Tree, why not simply come out with it and tell him? Why keep it a secret, especially now that they were together so frequently? He shook his head. Caroline could not possibly be Miss Tree. It made no sense.

He pushed into his study. The tenant's baskets sat stacked against the wall. He sat down in the chair behind his desk, staring at the baskets. Perhaps if he stared long enough, they would deliver themselves.

He had chosen to stay at Wirksworth yesterday after Montjoy left. After the fiasco under the kissing ball, Peter was not sure if Caroline was speaking to him let alone desirous to see him. And when he thought of the assertions Montjoy had made about her, Peter was not certain of his own feelings anymore. It left him feeling confused and quite frankly, muddled.

But had she not promised to deliver the baskets with him and help prepare for the servants' ball? She had made that promise before things had become awkward and uncomfortable between them.

Peter ran his hand through his hair. When had he become such a coward? The awkwardness would not just disappear. He needed to move past it. What better way to do that than to fetch Caroline and have her fulfill her promise? Perhaps then everything would return to normal.

He found Porter inspecting the footmen and their livery. "Porter, please have the sled ready as soon as possible." The fresh snow on the ground made the carriage an impractical choice.

"Walter, please fetch the baskets from my study and get them ready for delivery."

Walter bowed. "Yes, my lord." He headed off to recruit other servants to help with the task.

An hour later, Peter was at the reins, guiding the horses toward Whitley Wood. As he rounded the bend of the path, the sun peeked out from behind a cloud, shining on the stained glass windows of the Whitley Wood Chapel. He slowed the sled. The colored glass in the window looked transparent in the sunlight and Peter smiled at what it must look like from inside. He had not gazed at those windows since he was a boy.

He pulled around the castle, guiding the horses over the bridge, stopping in front of the staircase. He handed the reins to the stable boy who had run in behind him. "I will be out shortly. No need to stable them, just yet."

The boy held the horses still, rubbing their noses and talking quietly to them.

Peter mounted the steps, letting his excitement for delivering the baskets push back the dread of speaking to Caroline.

He lifted his hand to the knocker but paused. Why was he so excited? Was it really delivering the baskets that made his muscles feel jumpy and his face ache from smiling? He did not remember that happening in the past.

The thought of seeing Caroline, while it made his stomach twist, it also made his smile widen and his checks ache.

He did not know if she would agree to come. But he hoped she would. His only consolation was that she had promised, and he knew her well enough to know she would not cry off when she had given her word.

He frowned. Perhaps she had not promised exactly, but she had agreed to come and help, and was that not the same as a promise?

Stanton led him to the front sitting room. Caroline sat in the curved window seat, reading a book. Lady Montjoy and the countess were sitting near the fire, embroidering.

They looked up when Stanton announced him. Peter watched

to see if Caroline would acknowledge his arrival. While she did not make eye contact, he was moderately satisfied that she looked at him from the corner of her eye.

It pleased him to see that Caroline had not joined in on the needlework. Perhaps their conversation on its treachery had been well served.

He walked over to where she sat in the window with her feet pulled up under her skirt. Her gaze flitted up to his but returned just as quickly to her book. Although, he could tell she was not so intently focused on it as her eyes continued to scan the same lines over and over.

He grinned and his cheeks ached even more. "Lady Caroline." His gaze flicked over to her mother, who was obviously listening in. "I came to ask if you were available to help me deliver the baskets to my tenants?"

Her eyes stayed on the book and Peter had to admire her determination. "I am sorry, Lord Rockwell, but I do not think I shall be able to accompany you today."

"But did you not tell me you would come? I need someone with experience delivering Boxing Day baskets."

She looked up at him with squinted eyes. "It is not so difficult a task, my lord. You simply take the basket and hand it to your tenant. Perhaps even wish them a happy Christmas." Her eyes dropped back down to her book.

That did not go over well. Perhaps as he had expected, but not as he had hoped.

"Caroline, if you told Lord Rockwell you would help, you will help. It is a matter of honor."

Caroline's narrowed eyes turned to a full-on scowl at Peter's upturned lips. "Very well, my lord. When do you wish to leave?" Her voice was terse and clipped. It should have deterred him, but he found he liked the challenge she presented.

"I have the baskets in the sled. We may leave as soon as you are ready."

She set her book aside with a huff. "Let us get this over with, my lord. I shall meet you in the entryway shortly." Her feet poked out from under her gown. "If you could please avert your eyes, sir."

Peter turned his back to her, happy she was to come with him, but disappointed it was only because she was forced to do so. Perhaps it would be best to wait until after the baskets were delivered to ask her about the preparations for the ball.

Caroline came down the stairs dressed in the same woolen dress she had worn to collect greenery. How she managed to change so quickly was a mystery. He had never known a lady to change her gown in less than an hours' time.

Yet another quality to recommend her.

She buttoned her pelisse and wiggled her fingers into her gloves.

Either Caroline could not wait to be finished with the task or she was just ready to be out of the house. He hoped for the latter.

When she looked up at him, Peter extended his arm to her. Caroline barely touched him, making him look to see if she had actually put it there.

They walked out to the sled. Peter looked at her. "My apologies, Caroline. But you will be required to sit next to me. I am afraid the rear seat is taken up by the baskets." Had he sounded contrite enough?

"Oh? If I did not know better, I should think it was a ploy to get me to sit next to you, again."

He twisted his head slightly to the side, looking at her from the side of his eyes. "But you do know better?" Did she think she knew better because she believed the rumors Montjoy had spoken of or for some other reason?

He handed her up into the box, helping her arrange the rug, then climbed up himself. "Are you ready, my lady?"

Caroline shrugged. "I suppose so."

He flicked the reins and set off slowly in the direction of the Wirksworth tenant cottages.

"Thank you for coming with me." Peter risked a quick glance at her.

"As you were kind enough to remind me, I did volunteer. I should not like to break my word."

He feared her coolness would be the consequence of forcing her to come. "I missed you while we were singing the the other night. Your soprano was painfully absent. Are you recovered from your headache?"

She bit her lip. "I am for now." Her voice took on a subtle edge. "But you know how sudden a headache can come on."

Was she giving him notice that she intended to cry off early?

Peter kept his eyes forward. "I am glad to hear you are well."

They arrived at the first house and Peter handed her from the sled. Caroline reached behind the driver's box and retrieved a basket.

His stomach fluttered. Why was he nervous about meeting the tenants? He and Eleanor had often visited them with their mother when he was younger. But this felt different.

He lifted his hand to knock, realizing he did not know who lived within. It had been so long, the chance of a new tenant occupying the cottage was likely.

A pretty young lady answered the door with a small child perched on her hip. She looked at Peter and her brow furrowed, but when her gaze caught on Caroline, she relaxed. "Lady Caroline. It is good to see ye. I hope your Christmas was well." She opened the door wider and motioned them inside a small, unadorned room. A bed and a pallet occupied one side of the room while a stove and table occupied the other. A small room off the back held two cows standing behind a double rail.

Caroline smiled warmly. "It was very pleasant, indeed, Helen. Is Jim feeling better?" She motioned with her head to the bed.

Peter turned his head slightly, staring at her. How did she know so much about his tenants?

Helen let out a relieved sigh. "Dr. Hastings says he will be well. He just needs rest for a few days." Moisture formed in the woman's eyes. "How can I ever thank ye enough for sending the doctor over?"

Caroline waved it aside. "I am glad Jim is on the mend." She smiled at the child in the woman's arms. "And how is little Jacob, here?" The child held his hands out to Caroline, and she pulled him to her, bouncing lightly. Chubby little hands grabbed at a curl beside her face. Caroline pried her hair free, cooing and talking softly to the child.

"He is well, as ye can see."

Peter was speechless. He had never seen a lady take so much interest in a tenant, and another's tenant at that. Not even his mother, whom Peter had believed the picture of Christian goodness, could ask after every member of the family, nor would she have lifted a strange child into her arms. But then, these people were not strangers to Caroline, only to him.

A warmth settled in his chest. She was indeed a surprise.

Caroline handed the child back to his mother. She looked at Peter and he stared back at her. She reached forward and grasped the basket hanging from his hand, gently shaking her head and handed it over to Helen. "Here is a small token from Lord Rockwell." Caroline nudged him in the side.

He looked at her. Why had she done that?

Caroline let out an exasperated sigh. "And he wishes you

much felicity in the upcoming year. *Is that not right, my lord?*" Her tone was low, her words forced through gritted teeth.

"Ohhh, yes," Peter stammered. "Yes, of course. It is my greatest wish." Lud, he sounded completely daft.

Helen nodded to him, a small smile tugging at her lips. "Thank ye, my lord. This is very generous of ye."

Peter shrugged off the woman's gratitude. "You have been good tenants. It is I who should be thanking you."

Caroline kissed her fingers and pressed them to the child's forehead. "We shall leave you now to enjoy Boxing Day."

Peter nodded. "We are resuming the tradition of a Boxing Day Ball at the main house. I should be honored if your husband and you would come."

Helen opened her mouth to object, but Caroline held up a hand to cut her off. "You may bring the children. There will be games and food for them as well." She patted Helen on the arm. "I understand if Jim is not up to it. If he cannot make it, send word and I shall come collect the children and take them to the party. Then at least Jim and you can have an evening to yourselves."

"Thank ye, my lady."

They stepped from the house and Helen closed the door behind them.

Peter turned toward Caroline. "How do you know Helen?"

Caroline shrugged, as if the question was a ridiculous one. "I have seen her about the village, and have checked in on her periodically, when I knew she or someone in her family was not well."

She motioned them on to the next cottage. "Come, we do not have all day, my lord. You have yet to prepare for the ball."

At every cottage they visited, a similar interaction took place. The tenant's children greeted Caroline with hugs and excited chatter. The parents thanked her for some act of kindness she had offered them.

When they emerged from the last cottage, Peter reached out and grasped her by the arm, pulling her to a stop.

"How do you know so much about my tenants?"

Caroline shrugged. "There was no one at Wirksworth to look after them."

Peter realized how much had been neglected by his absence. He also realized there was much he had overlooked in Caroline. His chest tightened.

She was just the kind of lady to make a perfect mistress for Wirksworth Hall. Was Miss Tree such a lady? He would not know until he returned to London. What if it turned out she was not? Peter remained thoughtful as they made their way back to Whitley Wood Castle.

He pulled the sled to a stop at the bottom of the wooden steps leading to the entrance of the keep.

Peter handed out Caroline and escorted her up the stairs and into the castle, her hand still barely touching him.

Once all the hats and coats were deposited with the footman, Caroline turned and moved quickly up the stairs.

Peter rushed after her. He wished to speak with her, if she would slow down enough to let him catch up.

He finally came even with her partway down the corridor. "Caroline, please stop."

She came to a halt but kept her back to him.

Was he supposed to speak to her back? Perhaps he should just forget the whole idea of her helping him prepare for the ball.

The idea sent a ripple of panic through him. If she did not help him, he did not know what he would do. It was too late to purchase bread or cakes. Most every shop in the village would be closed. That would mean asking Mrs. Pratt to cook for the ball, and Peter loathed that option. Today was to be her day off—all the servants' day off. He could not take that away from them.

When he said nothing further, she turned around. "Yes, my Lord?" Her voice sounded impatient and expectant.

Peter sighed. "Why must you be *my lording* me? What have I done that you do not wish to be in my company?" He lowered his voice. "Is it because of the kissing ball? I can explain that."

Her cheeks colored and she straightened her back. "I have no problems with you, my lord. It is only, I understand that you are soon to be married. I do not wish to interfere with your upcoming nuptials and thought it better for us not to spend so much time in each other's company."

Peter pushed his lips out with a sigh. It seemed she had heard the rumors. But at least this was something he could refute. "There are no upcoming nuptials, Caroline."

Caroline took a step closer, her chin raised high. "There is no Miss Babineaux? I know you brought her to London. You told me yourself you had lived with her family while in France. It would not be proper for me to spend so much time with you. Especially unchaperoned."

Peter ran a hand through his hair. Gah. The infernal woman. Had he known what a problem Gabrielle would cause him, he would not have made the promises he did to Monsieur Babineaux. He closed his eyes. This was not Gabrielle's fault. She did not deserve his irritation.

"Gabrielle is not my fiancée."

Caroline's brows rose slowly into her hairline. He assumed it was the use of Gabrielle's Christian name. "We are not engaged nor are we to become so."

Peter ran his hand along the back of his neck. "It is a misunderstanding. The *Ton* does not know the circumstances nor the relationship. I look on Gabrielle...on Miss Babineaux, as I do Eleanor."

Caroline stood with her right hip jutted forward, her arms folded across her chest.

"When I was living with them in Lyon, Monsieur Babineaux expressed his concern for his daughter. He was old and he feared he would die before he saw her properly settled. I told him I would see to her welfare, should something happen to him."

She squinted at him, as if trying to assess the truthfulness of his story.

"As it turned out, he was correct to worry."

Caroline lifted her chin higher. "Why does it fall on you? Does the girl not have any family?"

Peter shook his head. "The mother's family disinherited Gabrielle's mother when she married Monsieur Babineaux. And there is no other family."

He assumed Caroline's same position. Why must she be so difficult? "Perhaps you would be convinced if I told you she is not yet sixteen. I could never marry the girl." Peter's nose scrunched up. "She is too much a little sister to me. But I will provide for her and see she is properly settled, just as I would my sister. I owe her father that much."

Caroline's face softened. Was she softening toward him or just in general?

She shrugged. "Thank you for telling me, my lord."

He reached out and grabbed her hand. Heat shot up his arm and left a tingling trail behind. He paused. Anxiety had never caused such a response. Could it be Caroline causing this reaction? "Wait. Caroline."

She glanced down at her hand in his then raised her eyes.

He did not believe she would accept, even after the explanation, but he had no choice. He must ask for her help.

"You had said you would come to Wirksworth today and help me prepare for the ball tonight." His words rushed from his lips. He gave her hand a small squeeze. "I do not think I can do it without you."

She swallowed and dropped her eyes to their hands again.

Peter released her. He did not wish her to decline because he had held her hand when she did not desire it.

"Please?" He was not usually one to grovel, but in this case, he would make an exception. "Please?" he begged again.

12

ah. Why had she made so many promises to him? Caroline remembered the closeness in which they had worked on Christmas Eve. It had been a moment of weakness. A moment of delusion where she thought he might have developed some feelings for her beyond old friends. But she had been wrong and now she would have to suffer the consequences.

"I will ask my mother first. If she has no objections..." Who was Caroline deceiving? She knew, just as Peter likely did, that her mother had no need for her.

"Of course. I should not think to deprive your mother of your help." Peter was at least kind enough to pretend that he thought there may be a likelihood of her presence being in demand here at Whitley Wood.

She entered the Yellow Sitting room, where her mother and Lydia were making plans. "My lady, Lord Rockwell is in need of my help at Wirksworth. If—"

Her mother waved her away. "Then go, Caroline. You are not needed here." *No, of course not. I have not been for many years.*

She stepped back into the corridor. Peter looked at her, a question in his eyes. "Well?"

She was certain he had heard the whole of the conversation. "It appears the fates are smiling down on you today, sir. I am free for the entirety of the day."

Peter's smile covered his face, reaching all the way to his eyes. He must be in very desperate need.

"I shall gather my things and meet you in the entry way."

Peter executed a very proper bow. "I shall be awaiting you, my lady." He turned and headed back the way he had come.

When she arrived at the entry, he led her out and to the driver's seat without hesitation. She felt a small thrill at the thought. Perhaps he did not think of her as simply an old friend. But would not old friends share a seat on a cold day? She slumped down and pulled the rug up to her chin.

They arrived at Wirksworth Hall and Peter handed her out while a stable hand held on to the horses. He led her around the house to the servant's entrance, guiding her into the large kitchen below stairs.

Caroline took in a deep breath as she stepped over the threshold. The room smelled of yeasty breads and sugary treats. The heat from the ovens and large fireplace seeped through her pelisse and warmed her to the bone.

Peter touched her arm. "If you would like, I can take your outer clothes and put them out of the way."

Caroline nodded and quickly worked the buttons loose. She handed him her pelisse and pulled off her gloves, tucking them inside her bonnet as she handed them over as well.

"Do you know what we shall be cooking?"

Peter held up his hand, just before he passed through a doorway. He returned a moment later. "Mrs. Pratt was good enough to leave some of her recipes here for us to use." He pointed to the top one. "I ordered the beef roast; it should already have been delivered. I thought we would start there?"

Caroline sifted through recipes, written in different hands and of differing stages of wear. It was obvious several of the recipes had been handed down for generations. "Yes. I think that would be best. Then we can start on the baking."

Caroline looked around the room and spotted an apron on the far side of the kitchen. She pulled it over her head and tied the strings at the small of her back. "You may wish to use one of these as well, Peter. Your valet will have a dickens of a time getting lard or meat drippings out of that fabric." She eyed Peter in his fine wool tailcoat and brocade waistcoat.

He walked to the hooks and pulled a white apron with a gathered ruffled edge over his head. He raised his eyebrows several times and Caroline laughed.

"It becomes you Peter, truly. Perhaps you could give up being master of the house and become Mrs. Pratt's assistant."

Peter smirked. "Perhaps we should see if I possess any culinary skills before we make such a rash decision."

Caroline nodded. "Perhaps that would be best."

She read over the recipe for the roast beef. "Where is the roast? Could you, please, locate it?"

Peter looked around, finding the wrapped meat on a counter in the cold room at the other side of the kitchen. He grabbed a pan as he passed by, placing them both on the wooden table in front of Caroline. She felt him standing beside her—very close beside her. It was difficult to concentrate with him being so near. "What herbs and spices do we need?" Caroline's voice wobbled slightly.

Peter nudged her. "I think we should abandon the recipe and flavor it on our own, do you not agree?"

Caroline looked up at him. "Abandon the recipe? Do you know what spices and herbs go well together?"

Peter shrugged. "I did a little cooking while I lived in France. I am confident with the meat, but the bread and pastries..." He gave a small shudder.

Caroline watched him while he unwrapped the meat. This man she had known for most of her life, was now such a mystery to her in so many ways. She did not know of any lords in England who would be at ease in a kitchen. He had not always been so open to such things; his travels had changed him—improved him in fascinating ways.

She took a step away from the meat in the pan. "I shall stand back and watch. You seem to have more experience than I."

Peter ducked his head. "When I traveled, I did not always have the luxury of living like an English lord." His mouth pinched together briefly. "Many times, it was safer, and I was treated better, if people thought I was a tradesman, as they were." His shoulders rose and then fell. "Jennings detested it. He did not play the role of traveling companion very well. But, the ruse helped me to learn many things I may not have been privy too, otherwise."

Caroline moved to the other side of the table and pulled a stool over. Sitting down, she leaned over and placed her elbows on the table. "It must have been glorious to live as someone besides Lord Creighton for a time."

"It was. Especially in the beginning." He looked over at her, pausing in his ministrations to the beef. "I left on the pretense of taking my tour, but I admit, I was escaping."

Caroline had figured as much after his third year of absence. She had oft times wondered if he would ever return home. "Is that why you stayed away so long?"

Peter shrugged. "Perhaps. At least in the beginning. But then I came to love the adventure of it all. A new place whenever I wanted to try something new or tired of the place I was currently living."

Caroline frowned at this new information. How could such a man be content to stay in one place, now that he was the Earl? It was one thing when his father was alive and overseeing all of the estates. But now it was up to Peter. From what he had just said, would he ever be content to stay in England? What about when he had a family? Would the time come when he was discontented with this life and he would move on to his next adventure, leaving everything—*everyone* behind?

Peter lifted the pan and turned to put it in the oven. Just as he stood to turn back, Porter walked into the kitchen. "Mrs. Pratt—." He looked at Peter and took a small step back. "My lord. I had no notion you were back."

Peter grinned. "We came in through the back door. It is supposed to be the servants' day of rest. And besides, we needed to get working on the food, if it is to be done before the ball tonight."

The butler swallowed and his brow furrowed. It was most out of character for the man. Caroline's stomach lurched.

"What is it, Porter?" Peter wiped his hands on a cloth.

"Your sister, Lady Kirtley and her family have come."

Peter clapped the butler on the arm and grinned.

Caroline's body relaxed.

Porter cleared his throat nervously. "She has brought Lady Rockwell with her as well."

Peter's smile faltered. "Lady Rockwell? What is my step-mother doing at Wirksworth?"

Caroline's stomach resumed its twisting and turned sour. Lady Rockwell had come. This was not pleasant news.

Peter had once been courting the lady, until she saw the chance to marry an earl sooner, rather than later, and married Peter's father instead. And only two months after the death of Peter's mother. The scandal had been widespread, but in the end, it was forgotten before his mother's mourning period had even ended.

While Caroline did not know for a fact, she believed Lady Rockwell had been the reason for Peter's hasty decision to take a grand tour.

"I have put their trunks in their usual rooms," Porter faltered. "Lady Rockwell insisted on her normal room—the one that now adjoins yours, my lord."

Peter nodded. "Please have Jennings move my things to a room in the guest wing, Porter."

"But my lord—"

"You heard me, Porter. Do it now." He removed his apron and set it on the counter. "Now, where did you say you put them?"

The butler swallowed again. "They are in the Ivy Sitting Room. I assumed you would not wish them in your mother's parlor."

Peter straightened his coats. "Thank you, Porter."

Peter turned to Caroline. "Would you care to accompany me in welcoming my guests?" His jaw was tight and rigid.

Caroline shook her head. "I believe this is a family matter and I should not be a part of it. I will continue working on the food while you are away."

Peter rubbed a hand over the back of his neck several times, raising and dropping his shoulders. Caroline could actually see the stress pushing down on him.

"Please, come with me." There was no question, just earnest begging.

Caroline knew this would certainly not turn out in her favor, but she found she could not deny him. Not when he looked on her with such desperation.

She untied her apron and placed it on the table, opposite of his. "Very well. If that is what you wish. But I cannot be gone long, or we shall not have time to bake all that we need to for the ball tonight."

Peter nodded, his chest rising and falling slowly as he took in several deep breaths. He was nervous about this meeting. Was it because he still held feelings for Lady Rockwell?

Even at thirteen, Caroline had seen the devastation in his face when he learned of his father's hasty marriage. It had nearly crushed Caroline's heart to see he had so completely loved someone else. Was she to stand by and witness a renewal of their affections for one another?

She caught Peter's eye and knew she would do just that, if Peter wished it. Even if it shattered her heart in the process.

❧ 13 ❧

Elizabeth *was here*. Peter ran a hand through his hair. No, Lady Rockwell was here. He had not thought of her as Elizabeth for a long time.

But why had she come? He knew she did not care for Wirksworth Hall, preferring the estate in Kent, or even the Rockwell townhouse in London.

Caroline stepped up beside him. He wanted to wrap her up in an embrace and thank her for facing this with him. But he refrained, instead only giving her a grimace.

She had been quite young, when the whole scandal with his father and Elizabeth had taken place. He doubted she even remembered it, let alone understood what it had entailed. But the notion that she would do as he asked, greeting Eleanor and Lady Rockwell with him, told of what a great friend she was to him.

He placed his hand on the small of her back to lead her to the Ivy Parlor. She stiffened slightly, but then she relaxed and allowed him to guide her from the room. Did she know how much comfort and strength she was giving him? He did not know if he could do this without her.

What had happened to the strong and confident man that had been here only moments ago? Elizabeth had always had that effect on him. He wished *Lady Rockwell* did not have the same effect.

They arrived at the door, and Peter paused. Must he really face her? Could he not send a note in with Porter and ask for Eleanor to come see him alone? Why had Eleanor brought her in the first place? It was not as if they had been dear friends. In all the letters he had received from Eleanor, she'd had had little to say of their stepmother.

He dropped his hand from Caroline's back. Was he ready for this? Was he ready to face Lady Rockwell, after all these years?

Caroline reached out and grabbed his little finger, giving it a reassuring squeeze. "I believe you can do this, Peter. But if you would prefer, we could bake a few things and come back in a little while."

Peter shook his head. "The sooner this is over with, the better I will be. Perhaps I can convince her to leave."

He knew it was a false hope. Lady Rockwell was never one to be forced into something she did not want. He grimaced. It said a lot about her role in marrying his father. She was also one who usually got what she wanted. But just what did she want this time?

Caroline let go of his finger and Peter wished to grab it back and hold on to her until this whole meeting was over. But he knew he could not. He just needed to get it over with and then they could return to their cooking in the kitchen. Just the two of them.

Lady Rockwell would never think of doing such menial work as cooking. Of that he was certain.

He even suspected it was the reason Eleanor had come to visit at just this time—so as to escape the task at the Kirtley estate. Although, he was not certain she had ever instituted the tradition in the first place. Eleanor never had enjoyed this part of the holidays when they were children.

He pushed the door open and stepped inside. His eyes immediately found his sister sitting on a chair by the fire.

It was a scene he remembered from his childhood. A sampler sat in her lap as her head turned toward the door.

Gabrielle sat next to Eleanor, her face screwed up as she concentrated on her needle work. He knew she still had a year before her come out, but she still looked like a child sitting there.

His sister stood when she saw him and quickly came to him, hugging him lightly. Eleanor had never been an overly emotional girl—too practical for such feelings. "Peter. It has been too long. Why did you not come and see us when you were in London?"

He shrugged. "After being gone for so long, I was busy. There was much to catch up on after father's death. And with my responsibilities in Lords...." He trailed off. It was a thin excuse, but he did not fully understand himself why he had not sought anyone out when he'd returned. He simply had not had a desire to do so. The only reason he had seen Montjoy was because he had come to see Peter first.

Eleanor dipped her head to Caroline. "Lady Caroline. It is good to see you. I saw you in London a time or two, but I regret we did not have a chance to talk."

Gabrielle, following his sister's lead, curtsied before him. "Good afternoon, my lord." Her accent was thick, but her words understandable.

Peter grinned at her. "I see Eleanor has been hard at work."

Gabrielle grinned and nodded. "*Oui.*"

He turned to Caroline. "Miss Gabrielle Babineaux, may I introduce Lady Caroline Trowbridge."

"It is a pleasure, indeed. Lord Rockwell has told me fondly of his time with you and your father." Caroline smiled at the girl, then glanced up at Peter. He thought there might be an apology in her eyes.

A swishing from across the room drew his attention away from Caroline and Gabrielle.

Lady Rockwell walked toward them at a sedate and graceful pace. Lud, she had not changed at all in appearance. The years had been kind to her.

Peter swallowed.

"Peter. How good it is to see you without your mask." She still purred like a cat when she spoke, yet somehow, Peter did not feel its affects as he once had.

His brow furrowed. Without his mask? How did Lady Rockwell know about the masquerade unless she had been there also? He looked at her. She was close to the same height as Miss Tree and their hair was a similar color. Not exact, but in the days since the ball, Peter could not say what Miss Tree's exact hair color was. She was blonde to be sure, but so was Lady Rockwell.

So was Caroline, for that matter.

He locked gazes with Lady Rockwell. Miss Tree's eyes were engraven on his memory. Surely, he would recognize them if he saw them again.

But as he stared at Lady Rockwell, the picture in his head became fuzzier, Miss Tree's eyes mingling with Lady Rockwell's. Or were they the same?

"It is a pleasure to be here, Peter."

He scrunched up his brow. Surely, he would have recognized her voice.

He shook his head, a dull thud forming at his temples. No. He could not let himself believe that Miss Tree and all her charms had been Lady Rockwell all along. It was unthinkable.

But what if Lady Rockwell *was* Miss Tree? Did that change his feeling for the mystery lady?

Peter frowned. It should, but now he was confused. In the small time he had been with Miss Tree, there had been something that drew him to her. But could he really be pulled toward Lady Rockwell? He had at one time, why should he not be again?

Elizabeth placed a hand on his arm and squeezed. "I am looking forward to beginning right where we left off, Peter."

Peter felt himself being lured into her charms. He took a step back, bumping into the table against the wall behind him. He could not figure this out right now. It would take more time than he presently had. "I am afraid that will have to wait. Car...Lady Caroline and I were in the midst of cooking the servants' feast for tonight's ball. If you will excuse us—."

Lady Rockwell closed the distance between them. "As mistress of this house, that responsibility falls to me, Peter. Do you not agree?"

He felt Caroline step away, as if distancing herself from what was coming. Why could she not stay at his side? He needed her even more now.

"I was not aware you were coming, as no note or letter was received. I have enlisted the help of Lady Caroline. Propriety would not allow me to dismiss her now, after she has so graciously given up her plans for the day.

Lady Rockwell moved between he and Caroline. "I am sure Lady Caroline has better things to do than help with a ball that is not even for her servants." She cast a look over her shoulder, eyeing Caroline from head to toe. "If she wishes to help, I am sure she could assist in decorating the ballroom. As for the letter, one was sent. I have no notion why you did not receive it." Her mouth turned down into a pout.

Peter's face heated and his hands balled at his side. "Lady Rockwell, you have only just arrived. I would imagine you are quite fatigued from the trip. Perhaps it would be best if you rested for now. You could help when you have awakened." He spoke through clenched teeth.

She shook her head and wrapped her arms around his, hanging on him like an ill-fitting coat. His stomach lurched, but not in the same way it did when Caroline had squeezed his finger.

"I find I am quite invigorated upon seeing you, Peter." She whispered in his ear, her breath blowing the hair curled at the back of his neck.

She grabbed him by the hand and pulled him toward the door. "Come, I am sure there is much to be done."

She cast a glance over her shoulder at Caroline and smiled condescendingly. "Your help is not needed any longer, Lady Caroline."

Caroline's cheeks pinked.

He tried to pull his arm free from Lady Rockwell, but she held tightly to him, pulling him to the corridor.

He looked at Caroline with wide eyes, hoping she would understand the apology there.

When they arrived in the kitchen, Lady Rockwell looked around. "Where is the cook? How is the feast to be done if she is absent?"

"Her name is Mrs. Pratt, Lady Rockwell." Peter sighed and scowled at her. "As I said, we are doing the cooking. I see you still do not listen fully to what I say. I suppose some things never change. Did my father mind that fault in you? Or did he simply overlook it?"

Lady Rockwell gave him her famous pouty smile. Had he actually found it seductive at one time? He supposed youth could do that to a man. Thankfully he had outgrown such tendencies while he had been away.

"I do not wish to talk about your father. It is you I wish to speak of." She tilted her head and looked down at her feet. "I never loved him. It was always you, Peter."

"I do not recall giving you leave to use my Christian name, Lady Rockwell."

"Ah, but I recall you doing precisely that." She smiled coyly.

He picked up the apron he had been wearing and put it over his head. "I am sure you think what we had was love. But I can assure you, you were wrong."

Lady Rockwell smirked at the apron around his waist. "You are cooking the food?" She laughed. "I thought you were simply saying it to drive off Lady Caroline. Heaven knows the girl is a homely little thing. It is no wonder she is destined to become a spinster." Elizabeth picked up the apron Caroline had been wearing with two fingers and looked at it with disdain. "I had no idea you were in earnest. But I suppose Lady Caroline was the right person to choose to help you. I am sure she has nothing better to do. Besides, a girl like that is bound to have spent a great deal of time with the servants."

Peter's jaw tightened. "Lest you have forgotten, Lady Caroline is the daughter of a marquess. You are the daughter of a baron. Perhaps you should remember your place."

Lady Rockwell shrugged. "It does not follow that she is desirable, nor that she possess the characteristics of a lady." She clucked her tongue. "Her marital status should tell you that much."

Peter now regretted taking on so much of this cooking. His head throbbed behind his eyes and he wished he could cry off, if for no other reason than to be out of Lady Rockwell's company.

He studied the recipe on the table. "If you insist on staying in here, at least make yourself useful and mix up the dough." He pushed a bowl towards her.

She looked at him as if he had asked her to play with a toad. "I will do no such thing. That is the work of a servant. I am not a servant." She pushed the bowl back to him.

Peter growled. "Did you not say you were the mistress of this house? In this house the mistress cooks for the servants' feast on Boxing Day."

Peter added the dry ingredients into the bowl and stirred them together.

"Perhaps it is time history changed. If you are so enamored with the idea, you do it."

Peter slammed his fist on the table. "I was doing just that, before you came in and drove Lady Caroline away." He shouted and she pulled back from him, not an altogether unpleasant turn of events. "Now I have no help. I cannot do this alone. Either help or leave the kitchen. You may yet be able to catch Lady Caroline and beg her forgiveness. But I refuse to continue arguing with you." His voiced dropped in volume, but not in irritation. Why would she not leave?

"What happened to you, Peter? You used to be fun. Now you are so serious and in high dudgeons. I just do not understand it."

He rubbed his thumb and forefinger back and forth above his brows.

"*Why* are you here, Lady Rockwell?"

She reached a hand across the table and placed it atop his. "I missed Wirksworth?"

Peter snorted, mixing the wet ingredients into the dry.

"Very well. I missed you. When I heard you were returned, I thought we might be able to begin again. We got on so well. Why should we not all these years later?"

Peter dumped the contents of the bowl onto the floured surface. He had watched Mademoiselle Le'Mont make bread frequently in Lyon. Surely, he could remember enough of the details now. He shoved his palms into the dough on the table pushing all his frustration into it. "That was before you jilted me and married my father."

Lady Rockwell waved his words aside. "That is in the past, Peter. I know we can get on well again. If you just give me a chance." She walked around the table and snaked her hand though his arm. "Come, do not tell me you are not interested."

"I am not interested." He pulled his arm away and continued kneading. "Now, please leave me and go fetch Lady Caroline."

She sighed. "I suppose we can continue this conversation later."

"Then you intend to stay?" What had he done to deserve such punishment? He must have displeased someone immensely.

"Come Peter, you do not seem pleased by the notion."

He kept his eyes trained on the yeasty ball on the counter in front of him, stretching the dough away from him and then pulling it back. "While you are not technically the dowager countess yet, I think it best, under the circumstances, if you remove yourself to the Dower House. I shall have Porter see to it immediately."

Lady Rockwell's mouth dropped open. "But there is no other Countess Rockwell. It is wholly inexcusable to force me from my home."

Peter laughed. "Wirksworth was never your home. You made your preferences quite well known."

"But—"

"I will not be deterred, Lady Rockwell. The Dower House is very lovely, and you should have the privacy one so recently widowed deserves."

"Recent? It has been nearly nine months." She scowled.

"And yet, the custom for mourning a husband is one year, at least." He looked over her light pink gown. "I see you have already discarded your mourning clothes."

Lady Rockwell pouted. "They were so dark and dull. Look at

me. I am a young woman yet. Why should I have to look like a doddering old woman just because my husband died?"

Peter shook his head. How was he to stand the next fortnight? Was Bedlam really so abhorrent? Compared to his present life, he did not think it could be any worse.

14

Caroline felt like a wrung-out rag. One moment Peter was laughing and joking with her, telling her stories of his travels and touching her in what felt like very intimate ways. The next he was avoiding kissing her or replacing her help with that of his step-mother and former fiancée. Her poor heart felt as if it had been stretched and tattered. If this is what it was like to be in love, it was no wonder people had avoided it for centuries and merely married for more practical reasons, like politics or business.

Caroline moved her breakfast about her plate. Her stomach seemed unwilling to accept anything served. It twisted and lurched whenever she thought on Peter and Lady Rockwell together in the kitchens of Wirksworth, working closely to get the food prepared. If old feelings were to surface, surely it would be under such conditions.

After leaving, she had returned home and shut herself up in the library. Everyone assumed she was still at Wirksworth, so no one had come in search of her. Caroline swallowed. She had told herself that was precisely what she had wanted, but if that was the case, why did she feel so lonely? Who did she truly have in this world who cared if she came or went? "Caroline, stop playing with your food and eat it. You are far too thin for a gentleman to find handsome."

The sharpness of her mother's words did not have its usual effect. She was too worn out to care today. "Yes, my lady," Caroline mumbled before taking an obligatory bite. She then continued to scooting the remaining food about her plate.

Her mother huffed but said no more on the matter. "I was surprised you did not even come home to change before the Wirksworth servants' party, Caroline. Lord Rockwell must have kept you very busy."

Caroline shrugged.

"How was the party? Was it well attended? Did even his tenants come?" Her mother placed her plate at the usual spot at the table and waited for the footman to pull out her chair. "I heard from Hill that his baskets were quite extravagant. They even included a small bag of coins equaling nearly a pound in each one."

Caroline nodded. "Lord Rockwell is a very generous man."

Her mother huffed. "He will be a broke generous man, if he does not curb himself. And with such generosity, his servants and tenants will expect the same, if not more next year." She placed a small bite of ham in her mouth and chewed. She swallowed and continued, as if she had never paused at all. "Not to mention, it makes the rest of us look miserly. It is bad form." She put another bite in her mouth. Her chewing became more pronounced. "I have also heard that someone had coal and food delivered to the poor in the village." Lady Killingsworth scowled and harrumphed. "I should think that was Lord Rockwell also, or rather, that is the name people are bandying about as being responsible." Only her mother could turn an act of charity into a disparaging comment.

Caroline put her fork down. As confused as she was about Peter and herself, she could not sit by and allow her mother to make such unkind remarks.

"I think one must keep in mind that the servants and tenants have been without a master in residence for nearly ten years. I think Lord Rockwell was generous and that it was not wholly undue."

"Oh, you think, do you? You were taught to keep your mouth shut when you had not the knowledge necessary to make decent conversation."

Caroline shrank back out of instinct, but then something clicked in her. She placed her serviette on the table. "I learned such behavior by your example, my lady. Perhaps it is best if you now take your own advice."

Her mother's mouth dropped open, fire smoldering in her eyes, but Caroline dropped a quick curtsy and left the room before her mother could regain her voice again.

She walked a little taller. Had she known it would feel this good to stand up to her mother, she would have done it earlier—much earlier.

She practically skipped down the corridor, a smile twitching at her mouth every time she pictured her mother's slackened jaw.

As she rounded the corner into the entryway on her way to the staircase, she nearly collided with Peter.

"Peter, my apologies. I did not see you there."

He grinned down at her. "I gathered that information on my own."

Her face heated. Why must she color up every time he spoke? "How was the Wirksworth Ball last evening? Did Helen come?"

He grinned. "She did come and brought the children, as well. Her husband was not up for the task, however, and stayed abed."

"I am happy she came. Did your staff enjoy themselves?"

Peter nodded. "I believe so. It was lovely, for the most part, though I did not approve of all those in attendance—" He looked as tired as she felt. "And I missed having you there." He looked at her tentatively. "But the servants seemed to enjoy it and that is the most important part."

Caroline nodded. She had thought herself in love with him when he was a spoiled child. But she could see now that it had only been a childish fancy. But now? There was so much goodness in Peter to love now. "I believe some masters forget that part. They believe it is another way for them to display to those around them." She clasped her hands behind her back and bounced on her toes slightly. "How did Mrs. Harris like her present?"

"She loved it; it even made her cry."

Lud, he was a handsome man, especially when he smiled like a little boy who had just been praised.

"And did she scold you for lying to her all those years ago?"

He shook his head. "No. She said she had suspected we had done something to the book, but she did not know what. She told me she appreciated me telling her what happened, even if it was twenty years too late."

Caroline wanted to hug him and tell him she was proud of him —of the man he had become—but she had used up all of her acumen on her mother this morning.

"How was the party here at Whitley Wood?"

Caroline nodded slowly. "It went well, or that is my under-standing. I did not attend. I found myself quite fatigued." From his furrowed brow, she did not think Peter believed her story.

He licked his lips and looked around the entryway. "I wondered if you, and Lord and Lady Montjoy, had plans this afternoon. The pond has frozen over. I am told we are able to go skating." He waggled his brows. "What do you say, Caroline? Are you up for it?"

Her stomach fluttered. "I have not skated in years. I do not know if I can even stay on my feet anymore."

His face fell. "Miss Babineaux, Eleanor and her family will be coming also." He bit his lower lip and Caroline glanced up to it. That was a mistake. Her mind conjured images of kissing him and Caroline felt even the tips of her ears burn.

"Will you come?"

His voice was quieter than normal, almost pleading, but sincere. She shook the thought from her head. Surely, she was imagining such things.

"You will not come?" Peter frowned down at her. "Why? Are you angry with me or uncertain about skating? If it is the latter, I promise I will keep hold of you."

The thought of Peter holding on to her nearly turned her knees to pudding.

"But if it is the former, please tell me so I may remedy the situation."

Little wrinkles appeared at the side of his eyes and between his brows. She tilted her head to the side. He was so easy to love. And that was certainly going to be her undoing.

❧

THE SUN PEEKED through the clouds, sparkling off the snow crystals on the ground surrounding the pond. Servants had removed the snow from the ice, leaving it smooth and white.

Caroline strapped the blades to the bottom of her sturdy winter boots. Pushing herself to standing, she tested her weight and balance on the skates. She pushed off lightly and glided a few feet out onto the pond.

Peter skated over and put out his arm to her.

She gave him an exaggerated scowl. "How is it you have not lost your skills at skating after all of these years?"

Peter grinned. "Who says I have not skated in years? I believe I found a pond or two every winter in whichever country I was in, except perhaps New Spain. It was far too warm there."

Before he and Caroline had gone more than a rod, Miss Babineaux skated over, laughing as one of Lady Kirtley's sons chased after her. She grabbed onto Peter's arm, circling around behind him, then she peeked out over his shoulder. A snowball sailed over, hitting Peter in the chest.

"Winston. I shall see you pay for that one, boy." Peter's voice was stern, but Caroline heard the note of playfulness.

Miss Babineaux laughed behind him. "*Excusez-moi*, Peter. I think that was for me." She skated out from behind him. "*Merci* for protecting me." Skating to the bank, she picked up a handful of snow and glided quickly toward Winston.

Caroline laughed. "I believe she will be quite the talk of London when she comes out. She is a delightful girl. I hope you are prepared for the line of suitors which are bound to be lined up at your door."

Peter grimaced. "Yes, Eleanor has hinted as much."

Samuel skated past, with Lydia holding tightly to his arm. It seemed she was not a proficient. Two of Lady Kirtley's daughters cut a line in front of them. Lord Kirtley shouted at his daughters, but it was too late. Lydia lost her footing, grabbing wildly onto Samuel's arm. He looked completely thrilled to have her holding him so tightly.

Caroline sighed. It would make her happy to see Samuel with a love match.

"That sounded heavy, indeed." Peter looked over at her as they neared the center of the pond.

Caroline was now confident in her abilities, but she was not about to inform him of such things. She was quite content with their current situation. "I am only happy for Samuel. I believe he and Lydia may yet have more than a marriage of convenience."

Peter nodded. "Yes, I was just noticing that also. He is a lucky man."

Caroline looked up at him. "Do you wish to have a love match or are you content in finding someone to further your political endeavors?"

Peter was silent for a moment. "When I left for my tour, I thought love a farce." He took in a deep breath. "But since I have returned, I have begun to think that perhaps love may be possible."

Did she dare ask? It would surely only lead to pain. But she needed to know. "What made you change your mind?"

"I met a young lady in London at a ball. The night before I was to return to Long Compton. She was...intriguing and mysterious. But I found myself drawn to her."

Caroline looked up at him. Was he speaking of her? Of Miss Tree? Her heart leapt at the thought that he could find her intriguing.

A gust of wind blasted into their faces, chilling her and bringing with it the realization that the intriguing part of Miss Tree was the mystery. Once he discovered it was her beneath the mask, there would be no more mystery. Nothing more to intrigue him.

Caroline suddenly felt the need for space. She was skating with him, thinking there was a chance for them. But she was wrong. She looked about. Perhaps she could feign a twist in her ankle and cry off.

Lady Rockwell launched herself onto the ice, her arms and legs flailing about her.

Caroline squinted, watching her. The lady's lack of proficiency seemed a bit practiced, as if the entire display was an act. But to what end?

She came full force toward them and Peter pushed Caroline to the side. Lady Rockwell reached him and wrapped her arms about his body, holding tightly, as if he were the only thing keeping her upright. A sly smile graced her lips.

Caroline nearly groaned out loud.

She glided about the pond as she had when she was a little girl, closing her eyes against the burning wind and breathing in the solitude she needed. If only it had not been Lady Rockwell's presence which brought it to her.

Peter caught up to her, matching his pace to hers. "You seem to have the hang of it."

Caroline nodded, his nearness bringing back all her jumbled feelings. "You appear to have freed yourself."

He shook his head and mumbled something about impossible women.

Lady Rockwell skated up beside him and grabbed his arm, pulling him away yet again. Why did she insist on always pulling him away? Caroline watched them through narrowed eyes. She did not like Lady Rockwell. Not even a little bit.

"It seems I warned you about the wrong lady. But still, I think you need be cautious." Samuel came to a stop just in front of her. "Lady Rockwell does not look like she will surrender easily."

Caroline swallowed. "Why are you so distrustful of him? He does not look as though he is enjoying the attention."

Samuel put her hand through his arm. "It is not him I am distrustful of. I was there when he courted Lady Rockwell. I know the effect she has on gentlemen. I am only trying to protect you."

"From being happy?" She had not intended to say it out loud. She looked ahead to Peter and Lady Rockwell.

Samuel followed her gaze. "I beg your pardon if I am wrong. But you do not look to be happy. I do not wish to see you hurt." He sighed. "More than you already are."

He patted her hand. "My wife is in need of my assistance, and as you seem to have regained your ice legs, I shall leave you to it."

Caroline nodded, but called out after him. "Samuel." He stopped and she closed most of the distance. "Thank you for looking out for me—for caring about me. I do appreciate you."

He grinned. "Someone has to. Heaven knows you are not doing very well at it yourself."

She looked back at Peter. Lady Rockwell still clung tightly to him. She reached up and ran her finger over the wrinkles at his eyes.

Caroline's stomach burned. Oh, how she had wished she could do that exact thing. But she never would, especially with everyone watching.

A cold wind blew, going right through her pelisse and wool dress. Caroline skated to the log at the side of the pond. She was cold and may as well return to the house. There was nothing keeping her here.

15

Peter scooted his chair around, not fully facing the window or the rest of his study. It allowed him to watch out the window while not putting his back entirely to the door.

A fresh layer of snow sparkled below the heavily overcast skies. He did not remember it ever being so cold and snowy as it had been of late. If only it had helped him in his plans to spend time with Caroline. Or at the very least, avoid Lady Rockwell.

The ice skating had not proven to be the adventure Peter had thought it would be.

When Peter had finally managed to disentangle himself from Lady Rockwell, he had turned in search of Caroline. But she was nowhere to be found, having left the pond without a word to anyone.

Peter's hand fisted on his desk next to him, knocking on the wooden top. The more Lady Rockwell had spoken to him, the more he doubted she was Miss Tree. Lady Rockwell lacked the wit and carefree nature to do such a thing. Besides, he doubted she would keep up the charade for any amount of time. She was under the delusion that she still had a claim over Peter, a notion he was quickly coming to discover was not true. Indeed, he had no notion what he had seen in her in the first place.

Caroline, on the other hand, when not under the thumb of her mother, displayed many of the same characteristics as Miss Tree. Although, it was still a possibility neither of the ladies were indeed the mysterious woman.

A quiet knock sounded at the door. Peter sighed. What could Lady Rockwell want now? Did she not realize this was his private space and he did not wish her here? "Come," he growled out.

Eleanor stuck her head in the door. "With such a greeting, it is no wonder people are avoiding you."

Peter grinned at his sister. She had been here for nearly three days and they had yet to talk privately. He had not realized how much he wished to speak with her until this moment. He stood and motioned her in. "Ah, Eleanor. Perhaps if you had used our secret knock, I should have received you kindlier." He motioned to the chair across from him. "Please, come in. We have scarcely had any time to talk since your arrival."

She pushed into the room and met him at the side of his desk. He placed a light kiss on her cheek. "It is odd to see you standing there rather than father."

Peter frowned. "It feels odd, I can assure you."

Eleanor sat down. "I confess. I had questioned whether you were happy about our visit or not. You have not seemed happy these past few days." She ran her hands down the front of her skirt as she spoke.

Peter smiled. It was good to see some habits never changed. He turned his chair so he could fully face his sister and sat down.

"It is not you. I am beyond pleased to have you and Kirtley here with the children." He shook his head. "Had I known what fun being an uncle could be, I should have returned years ago."

Eleanor smiled. "I tried to tell you you would like them. Although, I was thinking you found them overwhelming. They are quite exuberant at times."

Peter laughed, as he thought back on the children flying across the ice yesterday. "They make me feel younger. I only wish you did not have to leave."

Eleanor folded her hands in her lap. "They shall be coming to London with us. Perhaps they will entice you to come over to Penderton House more often. I think it very good for them to get to know the brother I have told them so much about."

Peter nodded. "I should like that very much."

Eleanor tilted her head to the side. "I confess, I did not think your mood was due to Richard and me, or even the children. It is not Gabrielle, is it?"

Peter shook his head. "I am happy she came with you. She seems to be enjoying herself. It is as if she has always been a member of the family."

Eleanor smiled. "I agree completely."

"You are daft, Eleanor. You know the cause." Peter leaned forward, placing his forearms on his desk. "Why did you bring her? I know you dislike her as much as I."

Eleanor shrugged. "It is true I do not think of her as a mother figure." She raised a brow. "She is five years my junior, after all. But in the past year, I have come to appreciate her for what she is —a young widow."

Peter shook his head. "Yes, well, she did not throw you over, did she?" He heard the anger in his voice. Why was he still angry? It had been ten years. He had thought himself over those feelings long ago.

"You are right, I do not have the same feelings for her as you do —as you did."

"No. And if my demeanor has been less than warm to you and

your family, I apologize. It was not my intention. I only wish she had not come with you. There is no reason for her to be here."

Eleanor worried at her bottom lip. She had something to say, but she did not know how to go about it. Peter smiled. Lud, he had missed this—having someone to talk with.

She gave a slight nod of her head, her forehead creased. "She is still mistress of this house, even if you do not wish her here." She glanced up at Peter. "Do you still have feelings for her, Peter? I believe that is her intention. I think she regrets marrying Papa and now thinks to right the wrong by marrying you."

Peter snorted. "It shall snow in Hades before I align myself with the likes of Lady Rockwell. She made her choice." Peter shrugged. "Besides, the scandal of marrying my step-mother? I haven't the constitution for it."

Eleanor sighed deeply. "I am relieved to hear it. I was ...worried."

Peter leaned back. "I can assure you my attentions are focused in a different direction entirely."

Eleanor raised a brow. "Oh? Pray tell, brother. Who is this creature that has captured your affections?"

Peter rubbed a hand over the back of his neck. He had discussed this with no one. Was he ready to discuss it now with Eleanor? He breathed in through his nose. She had been in London. Perhaps she had heard something which could solidly confirm Peter's suspicions.

"I met a lady at Lord Trenton's masquerade just before I left London."

Eleanor's eyes lit. "I was so disappointed to decline the invitation, but Richard was insistent we set out for Kent immediately after Parliament closed." She looked wistful. "Tell me, was it as enchanting as it sounded?"

Peter grimaced. "Enchanting? What do I know of enchanting?"

Eleanor chuckled. "Oh, yes. I forgot to whom I was speaking." She motioned to him with her hand. "Please continue."

"She was masked, of course, but I have never been so intrigued by a woman."

Eleanor leaned forward. "Do not keep me in suspense. What is the lady's name?"

Peter shrugged. "That's just it. I do not know. She refused to give it to me—only told me to call her Miss Tree."

Eleanor frowned. "Miss Tree? I do not believe I know of the lady."

Peter tilted his head to the side and smirked. "Miss Tree... mystery." He looked at her with wide eyes. Surely Eleanor was quick witted enough to get the joke.

Her eyes widened. "Ah, Miss Tree." She smiled. "The lady has some wit about her, does she not?"

Peter nodded. "Indeed. It was what captivated me at first." He interlaced his fingers on the desk. "When we danced, I asked her questions, but she was vague in her answers. Truly, I had no notion who she was...is."

Eleanor's brows raised.

"But I have my suspicions. It is not confirmed, but since arriving, things have begun to fall into place, and I believe I know her identity."

She scooted to the front of her seat. "Who is she? She is here? In Low Compton?"

Peter sighed. "I am not completely certain, but I believe Miss Tree is actually Lady Caroline. She was dressed as a peacock, with an iridescent green and blue mask and peacock feathers." He bit the inside of his cheek. What would Eleanor think of his admission? Would she think him daft? Eleanor was three years older than Peter, making her ten years older than Caroline. Eleanor had had very little to do with Caroline when they were growing up. Indeed, she had been married and moved to Kent when Caroline was only seven.

Eleanor looked pensive. "Now that you say it aloud, I believe I can see it. She was quite a lively child, if I remember correctly."

Peter nodded. "As I said, I am not certain I am correct."

"Have you come out and asked her?"

Peter slowly shook his head. "No. I have hinted, but what if I tell her how very intrigued I am with her and it turns out I am wrong? What would I say then?"

Eleanor leveled her gaze at him. "What are your feelings for Lady Caroline, apart from Miss Tree?"

He shrugged. "I am drawn to her, of that there is no doubt. But a part of me does not wish to give up the possibility of Miss Tree. What if I am wrong about Caroline? What if Miss Tree is the lady I am destined to be with, and not Caroline?"

Eleanor gave him a flat look. "Did you not believe you were destined to be with Elizabeth? We know how that turned out. Have you not, yet, given up the silly notion of destiny?"

Peter scowled at her. "Perhaps I misspoke, and destiny was not the correct word. I just do not want to choose the wrong lady. *Again.*" He sighed.

"But how do you know that this Miss Tree is, indeed, the right lady for you? You do not even know her. What if she is already married or betrothed?"

"That is why I need to find her. Then I could determine her character and make the right decision."

Eleanor sat back in her seat and folded her arms across her chest. "How certain are you that Lady Caroline and Miss Tree are the same person?"

"At times I am certain, but then I find a reason to doubt my belief. I convince myself that it is not possible—that I am not so fortunate." He leaned forward onto his desk and placed his face in his hands. "*If* Miss Tree is, indeed, Caroline, why would she not have simply told me already?"

Eleanor shrugged, her face full of condolence.

Peter thumbed the edge of the ledger sitting at the side of the desk. "I only need find a way to figure it out completely, so as to have no doubt."

Eleanor put her index finger to her pursed lips. Her eyes lit and she smiled. "I have it. Why do we not make the annual Twelfth Night Ball a masquerade? Perhaps Miss Tree will make an appearance and you will have your answer."

Peter slapped the desk and shot to his feet. "Eleanor you are a woman of great intelligence. That is a splendid idea. We should get the invitations out immediately." He stood and walked around the desk, placing another kiss on his sister's cheek.

She laughed and stood up. "You are a ninny at times, Peter. But I am glad you have returned. I missed you."

He looked down at her. "And I you." He paced to the fireplace, clasping his hands behind his back.

"I hope Lady Caroline *is* Miss Tree. I should like to see you happily settled, Peter."

Peter nodded, his muscles twitching. He had never hoped for anything more in his life. "Yes, it is my hope as well."

❦ 16 ❦

Caroline tied the ribbons of her bonnet under her chin. She caught her reflection in the mirror and lifted her face, tugging the bow a little tighter and straightening it at the same time. She turned her head to the side, looking at her silhouette. She thought of her thirteen-year-old self, in comparison to the woman looking back at her. She could understand how Peter had overlooked her all those years ago. But what about now? Did Caroline possess any features that would lead Peter in her direction, rather than Lady Rockwell's?

A person would have to be daft, indeed, to not see the purpose behind Lady Rockwell's visit.

Caroline frowned. Despite what her mother told her, Caroline knew she was moderately handsome. Gentlemen had told her such before. But then it could have been her dowry they found appealing, rather than her.

She pinched her cheeks. Her face had lost its baby fat since Peter saw her all those years ago, giving her high cheekbones and a rather graceful neck. Lady Rockwell also possessed such features, but with a feminine figure to match. Additionally, she knew the art of allurement, something Caroline did not think she could do, even if she knew how. Her cheeks pinked just thinking on it. What would Peter think of her if she were to sidle up beside him and wrap her arms around him? She knew she did not dare find out.

"We have not even moved outside into the cold, and already your cheeks are pink."

Caroline shifted her gaze in the mirror and noticed Peter standing behind her. He wore an easy smile and looked very handsome in his navy-blue tailcoat. He held his beaver tucked under his arm. She had not known Samuel had invited Peter to come along. In point of fact, she was quite surprised by it. Samuel had seemed quite disapproving of Peter since his return, so it did not follow that he should extend an invitation. It was likely the hunt would stray onto Wirksworth lands. Perhaps that was the reason Samuel felt inclined to invite Peter. Or maybe Samuel was simply afraid of Peter feeling slighted.

Whatever the reason, it let loose an entire swarm of butterflies in Caroline's stomach. She shifted her gaze back to the bonnet and moved it slightly to the right. "The thought of spending the day out of doors must have brought the color to my cheeks." Caroline turned around, coming face to chest with Peter. When had he moved closer? Usually she felt it when he was so close to her.

"You seem surprised to see me. Did Samuel not tell you I would be joining the hunt?"

Caroline shook her head. "He need not have done so. He is the Master of this hunt. I am only coming along to watch the excitement."

Peter smiled. Was he glad she was coming along or was he merely smiling because it was the polite thing to do?

"Samuel's invitation said we were to meet in the North

Morning Room." Peter held out his arm. "Would you do me the honor of allowing me to accompany you there?"

Caroline tried for a disinterested smile, but she could tell she failed miserably. She was certain he could read her feelings for him, as they were surely evident in every look she gave him.

"That is most kind of you, my lord." She placed her hand on his arm and they moved down the corridor.

"I must admit, I am quite excited for this hunt. It has been ages since I have been on one."

"You never hunted during your travels? With Monsieur Babineaux perhaps, or Herr Schöenbacher?"

Peter chuckled. "Monsieur Babineaux could not mount a horse, much less ride one in a hunt."

Caroline smiled. It was hard not to when he laughed his deep, throaty laugh. It was the same laugh she remembered from their youth, albeit much deeper now than it had been when Peter was a child.

"I confess, I have not been on one in quite some time, either."

Peter looked down at her. "Oh? Why not?"

Caroline shrugged. "There was no draw. I found myself rooting for the fox and hoping he would elude the pack." She caught his eye. "Samuel decided I was not welcome to come anymore, unless I could show my support for those who truly deserved it." She gave a bland raise of her brow.

"But you found someone you could support today?" His face brightened and he pulled her a little closer to him. Caroline shook her head. What a silly notion. Why should he pull her closer?

She stepped on the hem of her dress and stumbled. Peter tightened his hold on her arm as she likewise tightened her grip.

Straightening up, she ran a hand down the front of her skirts. "No, it is nothing like that. I find I have been indoors too much the last few days. I thought the fresh air would do me good."

Peter nodded his head, his mouth turned up to one side. "Yes, I am sure it will be just what you need."

They pushed into the morning room and Caroline's mood sank. Lady Rockwell sat in a chair near the large fireplace across from Lady Kirtley. Lord Kirtley stood near the fireplace. Why had she assumed it was only Peter who would be attending the hunt? It was only proper for Samuel to invite Peter and his guests.

Her mother and Lydia stood to the side. Lydia was dressed for the weather, but her mother was still in her morning gown.

Caroline dropped her hand from Peter's arm and walked over toward them. "Good morning, my lady. Are you not to join us on the hunt today?" Caroline looked around the room, noticing for the first time her father's absence. "Is Papa not participating either?"

Her mother shook her head. "Only a complete dolt would even consider taking your father out in such weather." Her mother frowned at her. "Please, Caroline. Think before you speak. Or better yet, do not speak at all."

Caroline kept her chin raised, earning her a glare. "My apologies, my lady."

She looked for Peter, but her stomach burned when she saw him sitting next to Lady Rockwell. She sat so close to him; Caroline could scarcely see any light between their bodies. As was the lady's tendency, one arm was wrapped around his while the other twirled the hair just below his ear at the back of his neck.

Caroline bit the inside of her cheek. She should cry off now, for surely this outing would not improve her mood. If anything, it would only sour it more.

Stanton carried in a tray with glasses and a decanter of brandy, which he distributed to each guest.

Samuel, dressed in his red tailcoat, raised his glass high in the air. "To success and warmth on this riding of the hounds."

Everyone raised their glasses and repeated, "to the riding of the hounds."

He grinned at the crowd. "Men, to the horses and ladies to the sled. The hounds are ready to get this hunt underway."

Peter stood up and was immediately captured by Lady Rockwell. He walked with her to the doorway, casting a quick glance over his shoulder at Caroline, but what he meant by it, she did not know.

Caroline met Lydia, Lady Kirtley, and Lady Rockwell at the bottom of the steps, flakes of snow falling softly around them.

The men were all mounted, the horses pawing at the ground in anticipation of the run ahead of them.

Mr. Willey and his two sons held the dogs on leashes, the pack barking and jumping about excitedly. The air all around them crackled with anticipation.

Harry handed all the women into the sled. Lydia sat next to Caroline, leaving poor Lady Kirtley to sit on the bench next to Lady Rockwell. Caroline did not miss the look of disappointment on Lady Kirtley's face.

Thomas set the sled going, following parallel with the men and horses. After a time, Thomas pulled away from the pack, moving slowly down the road and turning off several rods before the road split in two directions.

The sled glided on the snow, crunching beneath their weight. He maneuvered around thick trees and low growing hedges, pulling them over the tops of the smaller ones. Finally, they stopped on the edge of a large clearing.

Caroline put her hand over her brow, shading her eyes from the glint of sunlight off the snowy ground.

Thomas turned in his seat, looking first at Caroline and then moved his gaze to Lydia, unsure who he should be addressing.

"My lady, this is where Lord Montjoy requested they meet you for tea."

Lydia nodded. "This will do very well, Thomas." She extended her hand for Harry to help her from the sled.

"Perhaps it would be best for you to stay in the sled until the rugs and tents are up? You will be warmer than if you are standing about in the snow." He looked as if he were bracing himself for a lecture, but when none came, he relaxed slightly and moved around to another sled. The same one which had accompanied them when they had collected the greenery. Several servants stepped from the sled and began to unload several large rugs and a canvas tent. They moved with precision, everyone having a job to do.

Before long, the tent was erected, with curtains hanging down the sides and tied back with cords. Chairs and a table were set up beneath it.

Harry came back to the sled and extended his hand to Lydia. "There are bricks at all the chairs, my lady."

Lydia smiled and allowed him to hand her out, her foot crunching through the crusted top layer of snow and sinking into the fluffy snow beneath.

When it was Caroline's turn, she stepped down into the snow and picked up her skirts, walking quickly to the rugs ahead. She walked around the table, running her fingers over the covering.

It had been many years since she had attended tea on the hunt; many of these rugs and place settings she had not seen in years.

A barking in the distance drew her attention away from the table. She walked to the edge of the rug, grasping hold of a support pole. She looked out over the forest; streaks of white and brown appeared briefly in between the gaps of the trees. The horses were close behind, running past the clearing and deeper into the woods.

Caroline sighed. It looked as if they would be keeping warm with bricks and rugs, instead of tea for the time being.

She felt someone slide in next to her. Turning her head ever so slightly, she recognized the heavy scent surrounding Lady Rockwell even before she saw her.

"How are you this fine day, Lady Caroline? We have scarce spoken since my arrival."

Caroline looked out at the forest. "Yes, I was thinking just that this morning." It was an easy lie to tell. But then were not all the niceties of society just lies wrapped up in politeness?

Lady Rockwell cleared her throat and Caroline glanced at her. She motioned with her head in the direction the horses had galloped. "Will you be attending our traditional Twelfth Night Ball, my lady? It is to be a masquerade."

Caroline's brow furrowed. She had not heard this news. Could the lady be offering misinformation for some unknown reason? "I would assume my mother has already accepted the invitation."

"Tell me, what costume will you be wearing? I am considering a white fox or a robin for mine."

Caroline bit her lower lip. "I only have one costume and I do not believe there is time to have another made."

Lady Rockwell tsked. "I should think you are right. What are you wearing so I might find you the night of the ball? I should like to have someone I know to speak with." She smiled in the way a cat might smile before it ate the mouse.

"I shall be wearing the peacock."

Lady Rockwell smiled. "I am certain you will be lovely, my lady." She turned and said nothing more.

Caroline's shoulders dropped and the fingers clutching the tent post changed from white to pink.

"I do not know what you said to her, but she appears far too content."

Caroline looked over at Lydia.

"Did you know the Wirksworth Twelfth Night Ball is to be a masquerade?"

Lydia nodded. "The invitation with the details arrived yesterday." She glanced in Lady Rockwell's direction. "Was she uninviting you to the ball?"

Caroline shook her head. "No. We were merely discussing our costumes."

The dogs ran past on the other side of the clearing. And Caroline turned, hoping to catch sight of Peter.

"Are you sure he is what you want? I know Samuel is concerned for you."

Caroline groaned loud in her throat. Did everyone know of her feelings for Peter? Did Peter know? Caroline remembered the kiss that never happened under the mistletoe and the humiliation rolled over her anew. Was that why he had pulled away? He knew her feelings and did not wish to mislead her? "I do not know of what you are speaking." The words came out sounding monotone and rehearsed.

"I only serve to warn you, as a dear friend and sister. Samuel is afraid Peter's feelings for Lady Rockwell may rekindle." She tilted her head to the side and Caroline had the desire to slap the look of pity from Lydia's face.

"Perhaps it is time you abandoned your childish affection and leave him to the likes of Lady Rockwell." Lydia's eyes slid over to the lady. "She seems less concerned about the scandal such an association may bring."

Caroline released the pole and pulled away. "Thank you for your concern, my lady." She patted her hand. "But your worries are unfounded."

She moved to the table and waited until Thomas came to help her with her chair. She sat down and ran her hands down the front of her skirts.

The sound of horses echoed in the back of her mind, but they could not overpower the warnings from Lydia. *Leave him to Lady Rockwell. Samuel is afraid his feelings may be rekindled.*

"I am famished. May we join you lovely ladies for some tea?"

Caroline heard Samuel's voice, but did not look up. Were all her favorite holiday activities to be ruined this year?

Lady Rockwell led Peter to the table, seating him as far away from Caroline as was possible. He glanced at her, but then turned and replied to something Lady Rockwell asked. She snaked her arms around him.

It did not escape Caroline's attention that this time, he did not wiggle out of her grasp.

❧ 17 ❧

Caroline cracked an eye open. What was that noise? She had thought it was only a part of her dream, but now that she was fully awake, the noise persisted.

She sat up in her bed and looked around. The room was dark, only deep purples and blues coloring the sky outside her window.

Ping.

Caroline threw back the covers and placed her feet on the cold stone floor, slipping them quickly into the slippers beside her bed. She padded over to the window just as something hit the pane.

She looked out and saw the silhouette of a person standing on the ground just on the other side of the mote that surrounded the castle. He took a few steps to the side and bent down quickly. Peter. She would recognize him even in the darkness.

His arm went back and a moment later something hit the pane again. She pushed open the window and whispered as loudly as she could without the threat of awakening anyone else. "Peter, what are you doing?"

The wind must have blown in her favor, because he whisper-shouted back. "Get dressed. I have a surprise for you."

She furrowed her brow. "But it is so early. Surely it can wait."

He shook his head. "You must hurry, or we will be discovered and then everyone will have to join us. Please?"

This was ridiculous. Was she really considering doing what he asked? Her heart gave a little jump and she knew she would do nearly anything he asked of her. She looked at the bell pull and decided against waking her maid. Surely she could manage the task of dressing on her own. She picked a thick wool dress that was neither gray nor blue but reminded her of a stormy sea. Or what she thought one might look like.

She slipped from her night gown and pulled her short stays from the bureau. With shaky hands she pulled at the laces, tightening them before tying them off with a bow. Her skin was covered in gooseflesh as she pulled the thick dress over her head. Reaching as far back as she could she managed the top five buttons from over shoulders. From behind, she managed two more. That left one button, still undone at her back. Caroline looked in the mirror and shrugged. She would be in her pelisse. No one would see that she had missed a button.

She quickly yanked the ribbon from the bottom of her plait and ran her fingers through her hair. Pulling it all back, she twisted it into a chignon at the back of her head. She looked at herself in the mirror and inwardly cringed. Her maid could have done a much better job, but her bonnet would cover the worst of it.

Snatching up her heavy boots, she tiptoed down the staircase and retrieved her pelisse. She slipped on her boots, just before sliding through the small crack in the front door.

Peter stood at the bottom of the stairs, droplets of snow glistening on his hair in the low hanging moonlight. He grinned at her. "I confess, I am surprised you agreed to come."

Caroline gave him a lopsided smile back. "As am I. I do not know what I was thinking. Nothing about this is proper."

Peter nudged her. "Are you not tired of being proper all of the time?" He reached out and took her hand. Even the thickness of her gloves could not prevent the heat that transferred from his hand to hers. It traveled up her arm and warmed the whole of her body. She was certain she was making more of this outing then Peter intended, but for this moment, she was going to allow herself to hope.

He led her out of the inner courtyard and across the drawbridge.

"Where are we going? I thought you said you had a surprise."

He pulled her along, always keeping her right beside him. "It is just up here a little farther."

"What are you even doing awake at this hour?"

He shrugged. "I could not sleep."

She grunted. "I was sleeping quite well, thank you. Perhaps next time you could awaken someone else when you are unable to sleep." She did not mean it, but did he know that? Her whole body was alive and aware of the man at her side.

He looked over at her. "Would you truly rather be in bed than enjoying this beautiful morning?"

Caroline snorted. "Is it morning? It looks to still be night."

He laughed. "I was afraid if I waited until it was light, we would not be able to do this alone." He glanced away. "It seems there is always someone around." He huffed and a cloud formed in front of his face. "Lady Rockwell, and even your brother, seem to always be under foot."

"What did you think so important that we need do it without a chaperone?"

They finally came to a stop at the base of a small hill. Caroline looked up at Peter, her brow creased. What was he about? She saw nothing surprising or special about this place.

Peter released her hand and she looked down, disappointment coursing through her. "Stay right here while I fetch my surprise." He hurried away, stopping behind a low stand of bushes. "Close your eyes until I tell you to open them."

Caroline leveled her gaze at him, her head dropped to the side. "I am not a child, Peter. Must I close my eyes?"

Peter's smile dropped. "Please? Just this one time will you do as I ask without arguing?"

Caroline sighed. "Oh, very well." She closed her eyes, feeling vulnerable. Why was he so insistent about this? Memories of their childhood flitted to her mind. She remembered Peter doing this very thing, only to run off and hide, leaving her standing alone. Her heart beat a little faster. "You are not going to run off on me as you did when we were children, are you, Peter?"

Silence filled the air and Caroline felt her muscles tighten. She counted to five and then cracked her eyes open. Peter stood barely a rod in front of her, his head turned back and something trailing behind him. Seeing he had not left her, her body relaxed a fraction and she closed her eyes tight.

She felt his breath tickle her cheek before he spoke. "You can open your eyes."

Her eyes slowly opened. Peter stood close to her, the puffs of their breath mingling in the air between them. His cheeks and nose were pink from the cold, but his eyes sparkled and crinkled at the corners as he smiled down at her.

She swallowed hard. "Where is this surprise you promised me?" Her voice sounded strangled and slightly high pitched.

Peter brought his hand forward. A rope looped around his fingers several times before dropping down to a small wooden sled.

Caroline's eyes widened and a squeal sounded from her lips.

"Where did you find it? I have not seen that sled in forever." Her eyes came up to meet his. "Not since the winter before you left."

Peter grinned. "I have thought back on that winter oft while I was away." He lifted the sled up. "It is smaller than I remember. But it feels sturdy enough." He raised his brows. "What do you say? Are you willing to have a go?"

She eyed the sled. It was much smaller than she remembered, but the tickle in her stomach told her she wanted to try. Caroline nodded. "Of course. Have I ever been chicken livered before? Why should I be now?"

Peter's face lit up and Caroline felt her legs swoon. How was it possible he was not married? Surely there were ladies from America to China who would gladly have accepted his offer. She frowned. Perhaps Samuel was correct—Peter was that kind of man. She shook her head. He could not be, her brain would not allow her to think such thoughts.

"Have you changed your mind? You do not look so confident now." His brow was furrowed to match hers. "You do not have to do it if you are not comfortable with the notion. I will happily walk you back to Whitley Wood."

Caroline pushed any worrisome thoughts away. "No. I have not changed my mind." She looked up at the hill. "I was only trying to decide which side would prove the most diverting."

Peter took her hand back in his. "I have already planned it out. Come."

Caroline laughed. "When did you do all this planning?"

He shrugged. "Did I not tell you I was having trouble sleeping?"

"You planned this all tonight?"

Peter shook his head. "Tonight is not my first sleepless night." He glanced at her. "It is only tonight I mustered enough nerve to ask you to join me."

If Caroline did not know him better, she might think him apprehensive just now.

They trudged to the top of the hill and Peter set the sled down, keeping hold of the rope. He motioned with his hand. "Why do you not get on first? That way I can keep the sled steady."

"Do you think we can both fit?" She looked at the small sled. She remembered the fit was tight when she was only a child. Now that they were both adults, it seemed doubtful.

He winked at her. "Perhaps not. But I think it shall be fun to try; do you not agree?"

Caroline shivered, even though her body was warm from head to toe. She nodded, because she knew her voice would betray her.

Peter kept hold of her hand as she stepped one foot over the sled and sat down. It slid under her weight until Peter curled the rope a few more times around his hand.

She looked up at him with questioning eyes. She knew his muscles were well developed, having noticed them under his tightly fitted coat. He was up to the task of holding her weight under normal circumstances, but the slipperiness of the snow added an obstacle.

"Sit down and put your feet on. I promise I will not let go until you are ready."

She eyed him. "Have you not used those very words on me before, only to let go of the rope and send me careening down the hill?" She had been no more than nine at the time.

Peter chuckled. "I had forgotten about that. But if you will recall, it was only after you called me a half-wit. I think the punishment fit the crime."

"You are saying if I do not call you names, you shall let me ready myself?" Her voice held skepticism.

"Precisely. Now, put your feet up and scoot closer to the front."

Caroline gaped at him. "But if I am too close to the front, I shall lose my balance and fall head over heels down the hill."

"But there shall not be room on the back for me, if you do not move forward." He gave her hand a squeeze. "I will not let you tumble down the hillside, Caroline. I promise."

Butterflies let loose in her stomach. He was determined to sit behind her? She had thought him in jest when he suggested it. Her mother would never approve, but the thought of sitting so close to Peter made her light-headed. She teetered slightly and he tightened his grip on her hand. "Are you well?"

She nodded, pulling her feet up and straightening her dress around them. She felt the weight of Peter's body as he settled behind her, his feet still keeping the sled in place. His arms went around her waist and she stopped breathing, unable to think or swallow.

"Are you ready?" He whispered in her ear.

All she could muster was a nod.

Peter picked his feet up and placed them at the side of her body. Caroline closed her eyes waiting for the sled to slip down the hill. But nothing happened.

She opened them in time for Peter to release one hand from her waist and press it into the ground, giving them a little push. The sled dangled on the edge for a moment before it tipped forward and started down the hill.

Tears hovered in the corners of her eyes as the wind blew past them. Peter's arms tightened, combating the cold that threatened to chill her to the bone. The sled reached the bottom and the right runner hit a bump in the ground, tossing both Peter and Caroline into a heap at the bottom.

She rolled to her back and opened her eyes, looking up at the slightly pinking sky. Peter moved beside her. "Are you hurt?"

There was genuine concern in his voice and Caroline nearly

melted into the snow. The tears from the wind, finally spilled over and burned a trail down the side of her face.

Peter's face appeared over hers, panicked and stricken. "Thunder and turf, what have I done? You are hurt."

Caroline shook her head. "No. I am well."

He moved back slowly, but his face still held worry. "You are certain? But you are crying. Why are you crying if you are not hurt?"

She pushed herself up to sitting, shaking her arms and her legs to try and convince him she was not harmed. "I am not crying. The wind is what caused the tears." She looked back up the hillside and laughed. "I have not had such fun in a very long time." She jumped up and extended her hand. "Come, Peter. Let's make another run."

He fell back into the snow, his whole body relaxing as the worry drained from his face. He reached out a hand and scooped up a handful of snow, tossing it at her before she had a chance to move out of the way. "Do not scare me like that again. I thought...." His face clouded over again. "Samuel would have my head if I let anything happen to you."

Caroline stared down at him. "You are only worried about what Samuel would do?"

Peter rolled to his side and pushed himself up. He stood in front of her and wiped at a stray tear as it ran down her face. The wind dried the wetness from his glove almost before his finger left her skin. "I would never forgive myself if I let something happen to you." Peter cleared his throat. "I am sure your father would see me hanged as well."

Caroline took in a stuttering breath.

Peter picked up her hand and gave it a tug. "You said you wanted to go again? Well, come then. It is nearly daylight. We do not have much time before I must return you, before your entire household knows of your absence and comes looking for you."

Caroline grinned. "Yes, that would ruin the purpose for this outing, would it not?"

He nodded as he pulled her to his side and they walked back up the hill, the sled trailing behind them.

They positioned themselves on the sled again and Peter wrapped his arms around her. Caroline shivered again. Why was she allowing herself to be so affected? She knew it was not wise, but she could not help herself.

"Are you cold?" He pulled her tighter against him, his breath warming her ear and tickling her neck. Caroline was not sure how much more of this she could handle, even as she never wanted it to end. But she knew it must and then what would she be left with? Her eyes closed. Memories had helped her through these last ten years of his absence, perhaps if she committed every detail of this time together to memory, she could use it to get her through the next ten years.

She shook head. "No. I am merely anticipating our next trip down the hill."

"Then let's go." Peter used his hand to push them off and they flew down the hill side, faster than they had the first time. The sled hit the same rut, flipping them upside down. Caroline landed with a thud.

She opened her eyes and found herself face to face with Peter. Her face heated when she realized she was on top of him, but her body refused to roll off. Even in her wildest, most private dreams, she had never allowed herself to imagine being this close to him. She felt her body rise with each breath he took. *Move off him*, her brain yelled at her body. But her body refused to listen.

He winked at her. "Ah, I wonder what I am to do to repeat that run?"

Caroline hit him lightly on the chest, her laughing coming out shaky and uncertain. "You are a rake, Peter. You know that?"

His smile faded and his eyes took on a serious look. He rolled her to the side and turned to face her.

She knew she should be cold, lying in the snow, but with the intensity of his look, she felt nothing but warmth and energy racing though her.

"Do you really believe that?"

Afraid he would see her feelings written all over her face, Caroline smirked at him.

He stared at her intently. "Please tell me. I must know your opinion of me."

She licked her lips and Peter's eyes followed the trail of her tongue.

She had received that very look from other gentlemen in the past, but none had made her feel the way Peter's look did now.

She shook her head. "No. I do not believe you are such a man."

His body relaxed and he leaned his forehead against hers. "I am happy for it. I do not think I could endure knowing you thought me a scoundrel of any kind."

His eyes dropped to her lips again and Caroline said a little prayer that this time he would follow through. Her muscles twitched with anticipation.

"There you are." The shout carried over the wind. Only then did the pounding of horse hooves separate from the pounding of her pulse in her ears. Samuel reigned in his horse as Peter leaned back.

Samuel furrowed his brow. "Did I interrupt something?" There was a touch of laughter in his voice.

Peter jumped to his feet, clearing his throat as he did. "No, not at all Montjoy. Lady Caroline was thrown from the sled when it hit that divot. I was merely checking her for injuries."

Caroline could hear the regret in his voice. Did he regret the intrusion or that he had considered kissing her in the first place? She lay her head back in the snow and closed her eyes, letting the cold seep through her clothing and into her bones. She felt tired and empty inside. Another chance for her to get some indication that Peter may love her had come and gone. No doubt he would never love her as much as she loved him, but she did not care. Just to have him love her at all was enough. But even that seemed to elude her.

"Yes, I am sure that is *all* you were doing." Samuel jumped from his horse and rushed to her side. "Are you hurt? Why are you not standing?"

Caroline pounded her fists into the snow next to her. "Gah. Nothing is wrong with me I am simply frustrated."

Peter's eyes widened slightly, and he grinned.

Samuel helped her up. "Why are you frustrated?"

"Because I am certain you are going to drag me back to Whitley and end this very diverting activity."

Samuel placed his hand at her elbow. "Of course I am. You are soaking wet and I can feel the cold even through my gloves." He looked at Peter. "What were you thinking? This plan was ill-conceived in so many ways. It is good I am the one Barton told of her absence." He shook his head. "Mother would be near apoplexy about this if she were ever to find out."

Caroline jerked her arm out of his grasp. "But she will not, will she Samuel?" She glared at her brother, angry that he was ruining her time with Peter again. But even more angry that he had disrupted the one thing she had dreamed about for more than fifteen years. "If you are ready, I should like to return home and take a hot bath."

She turned to Peter. "Thank you for a lovely time."

He opened his mouth to say something, but Samuel steered her away and led her to his horse.

She allowed him to lift her up to the saddle before he hoisted himself up and settled in behind her.

Caroline could not help but wish it was Peter putting a hand around to steady her.

Samuel turned his gelding back toward Whitley Wood. "What were you thinking, coming out here alone with him?" He sighed. "And sledding? What if something had happened to you?"

"Nothing ever happens to me." Caroline sulked. She looked at Peter from over Samuel's shoulder. "Besides, Peter would never let anything happen to me."

❧ 18 ❦

Peter stared after Montjoy's retreating horse. His throat felt tight and he shivered. But even with the cold seeping through his clothes, he had no energy to move or return to the house. He sat down on the sled and dropped his head into his hands.

Never had he felt such a feeling of completeness as he had felt just now with Caroline. He had never felt this way about anyone—not even Miss Tree made his whole body feel so alive.

He took in a stuttering breath and the cold burned his throat and lungs. He loved Caroline. His desire to know the identity of the mysterious lady in the mask was no longer important. If it did, indeed, turn out to be Caroline, all the better. But if it was not, he truly did not care. Caroline was the only one he wished to be with.

He closed his eyes, reliving the moment when their breaths mingled, and he was inches away from kissing her. Then he heard Montjoy's voice, almost as if he were standing there. Why did the man keep ruining his chances to kiss her? "Dratted fool." Peter thought they had come to an agreement the other day.

He sucked in a long, burning lungful of air and pushed himself up. He reached down and grabbed hold of the rope, tugging the sled behind him as he trudged back to Wirksworth. The walk seemed much longer than it had only a few hours earlier.

What was he to do with this newly discovered information about his feelings for Caroline? He wanted to race to Whitley Wood and declare himself to her at that moment. But he held himself back. He had awakened her very early and she would no doubt be very cold when she arrived home. He guessed a warm bath and sleep were likely her immediate plans.

He hunched his shoulders and gathered his greatcoat closer to him. He had to admit, a warm bath did sound enticing. But the thought of even another day without Caroline with him made his chest hurt and his spirits sag.

The Twelfth Night Ball was tomorrow. Would it not be more memorable if he should ask for her hand at the ball? He increased the length of his steps, each one feeling lighter than the last. It would be torture to wait another day entirely, but he believed it may be worth it.

If things went according to his plan, he would find her in her peacock mask and lead her to the kissing ball. Then he would not allow anyone to stop him from kissing her. Not Samuel. Not Lady Rockwell. Perhaps he should enlist Eleanor's help to that end.

Once he had finally kissed her, he would ask for her hand.

A large smile covered his face as he pushed open the kitchen door. The heat hit him full on and it felt as if a thousand pins were pushing into his skin. He worked his jaw, opening and closing his mouth, trying to work the blood into his cheeks. Mrs. Pratt bustled in from the larder, her arms loaded with flour and other ingredients. Her eyes widened when she saw Peter standing just inside the doorway.

He stepped forward. "Let me help you with that, Mrs. Pratt."

He took several of the larger bundles from her load and placed them on the large table in the center of the room.

She set the remaining items in her arms down and ran her hands down her dress as she curtsied. "My lord. I was not expecting you. Is there something I can do for you?"

Peter smiled. "No. I was freezing, and this door was the closest. I am sorry for intruding on your breakfast preparations."

She placed a hand to her hair, pushing at the curls hanging down from her mobcap. "It is no intrusion, my lord." She motioned to him. "You look very cold, indeed. Your nose and cheeks look like cherries they are so red. Let me make you some tea." She glanced at the stove. "And the biscuits should be nearly ready."

Peter dipped his head slightly. "Thank you, Mrs. Pratt." He pulled out a stool from under the table and sat down.

Her eyes widened. "Do you not wish to sit in the breakfast room, my lord?"

Peter shook his head. "Only if you make me. I have missed some of the informalities that I participated in while I traveled. When I was in America, I stayed with a family and we would eat about a table in the kitchen for every meal." He rested his elbows on the table and dropped his chin into his hands. "There were more than just stoves providing warmth in that home. I miss that closeness at times."

Mrs. Pratt smiled tightly, and Peter could tell she was not comfortable with his presence. "How long have you been employed here, Mrs. Pratt?"

She took up the corner of her apron and began to twist it. "Nearly four years, my lord."

Peter nodded. Most of the staff he knew from before he left. There were the few maids and other lesser positions that he did not know. But Mrs. Pratt was the only servant with authority that he did not know from before his travels.

She shifted. "Have you been displeased with my work, my lord?"

Peter put up his hands in protest of her words. "No. Quite the contrary. You were hired while I was away…"

She stared at him.

Perhaps today was not the day to forge a relationship with this servant. But it did not follow that he would give up. He just needed to take it slowly. He scooted out from under the table and stood up. "I have changed my mind. I believe I will take my tea and biscuit in my chambers. Would you please be so kind as to heat water for a bath? I do not think I shall get warm any other way."

Mrs. Pratt visibly relaxed and nodded. "Right away, sir. I will send up your tea with Jennings."

Peter pushed the stool back under the table. "Thank you, Mrs. Pratt."

Peter took the back stairs to his chambers, but still Jennings managed to arrive first, the tea tray already situated on the low table by the newly stoked fire.

Peter stood while Jennings removed his coats and then sat down hard in the chair. How could he be so exhausted this early in the day? Perhaps he would follow Caroline's lead and rest after he'd had time to make his plan for the ball while in his bath.

JENNINGS BRUSHED at Peter's tailcoat. He finished and set it aside, giving Peter's coat one last tug. He held up a fur covered mask. "Shall I tie it on, my lord?"

Peter shook his head. "No. I can do it before I enter the hall. I do not wish to wear it any longer than is necessary." He ran his finger over the fur. "The dratted thing itches like the dickens." He tucked the mask into his coat pocket. "Next time I am in need of a masquerade costume, please remind me to pick something less furry. Perhaps a turtle, or some such thing would be preferable."

Jennings nodded. "Of course, my lord. No fur." Peter stared at him. Sometimes he wished Jennings was not so formal. Even when they had been traveling, the man had been stiff and cold.

Peter took one last look in the mirror and his pulse picked up. Tonight was the night he would ensure Caroline was to be his forever. Suddenly, he could not wait to get to the ballroom. "My gloves, Jennings."

The valet placed brown gloves, with the same brown fur as the mask sewn to the tops, into Peter's hands.

Peter looked down at them. "Well, if nothing else, I shall be warm tonight."

"And very dashing, my lord."

Peter nodded and shooed the man away. "Yes, well there is only one lady I care about impressing," he mumbled.

"I am sure Lady Caroline will find you most handsome, sir."

Peter's gaze jerked up to his valet. "What do you know of Lady Caroline?"

"Nothing, sir." He trailed off and began to pick up the discarded clothing from the floor and chairs.

"Is this what is being bandied about below stairs? You've never been one to listen to gossip, Jennings."

The man shook his head. "There is no gossip below stairs about Lady Caroline, sir. Most of it is about Lady Rockwell."

Peter's brow rose. "Oh? What is being said of her?"

"Only that she is here to try and win back your affections."

Peter flicked his eyebrows up quickly and shrugged. The servants usually had the right of it. "Then why did you mention Lady Caroline?"

The valet continued straightening the room. He paused for a

moment as if thinking through his words carefully. He had always been a smart man. It was one of the reasons Peter had dragged him along on his extended tour. "I know you are hoping to ask for her hand. I only assumed it would be tonight, which I understand was not my place to do. I apologize, my lord."

Peter stepped back. How did he know this? Peter had not even told Eleanor what he had discovered while sledding. "How did you come across such information?"

Jennings stared at Peter. "You have begun talking in your sleep these past few nights." He flicked his gaze to meet Peter's widened eyes. "I have spoken of it to no one, of that you have my word. You know I would never betray your trust."

He talked in his sleep? How long had that been going on? He had never been told of it before. "How long has this been happening?"

The valet picked up Peter's Hessians and tucked them under his arm as he grabbed another article off the floor. "Only these last few nights, my lord. I have never heard you do it before."

This was something to think about, but not now. He had more pressing things to think about tonight.

Peter left his chambers and headed down the stairs to the ballroom. Eleanor stood just inside the door, ready to receive their guests. Peter's lips turned up. His sister was just as lovely as ever. Kirtley stood beside her, his hands clasped behind his back.

Peter placed his mask over his eyes and tied it as he walked toward them. "Where is Lady Rockwell? As the mistress of this house, should she not be here to greet our guests?" Peter's annoyance was obvious.

Kirtley raised a brow and gave a slight shake of his head. Peter realized too late that he should not have brought this subject up.

Eleanor huffed. "She is not ready yet. Besides, it is not as if she knows anyone here. 'Peter and you can manage the receiving line.'" Eleanor's nostril flared as she mimicked Lady Rockwell's throaty voice.

Peter gave a half smile. The impersonation was very good. If he were not so irritated by Lady Rockwell's obvious dismissal of propriety, Peter would have laughed out loud.

Thomas arrived with the first guests and Peter pushed down his anger, instead putting his energy into greeting his friends and neighbors.

Hours after the ball began, Peter still had yet to see Caroline. Her parents had arrived with Lord and Lady Montjoy, but Caroline had not come with them. Lady Killingsworth had alluded to the fact that Caroline had not been ready to leave when the carriage was to depart, so she had been left behind.

Peter's hopes sank. Would she not be coming at all? How could she miss this ball? How could she miss seeing him? Perhaps he had misread her and she was not as amiable toward him as Samuel implied. It was the first time he had worried that perhaps his attentions would not be welcomed.

Peter milled about the crowd, talking with people and catching up on missed time, but his gaze was constantly moving about the room, searching.

Eleanor and Kirtley stood talking to a crowd and Peter moved in their direction. As he neared, the orchestra played the first notes of the next set. A grouping of people moved to take their places.

Peter stopped beside Eleanor. "Have you seen our step-mother yet?"

Eleanor shook her head and glanced at him. "Put a smile on your face, Peter. You look as if you have been sucking on lemons."

He smirked at her. "Better?"

She shrugged. "Can I assume from your mood you have not seen Miss Tree or Lady Caroline?"

Peter shook his head. "In truth, I care not if I find out the identity of Miss Tree. I had only wanted to see Caroline. I wished to speak with her about something quite important."

Eleanor grinned and nudged his arm. "If you wish to ask her what I believe you do, I am very happy for you, brother."

Peter scarcely heard the last words. A glimmering blue and green dress caught his eye at the far side of the room. Her back was to him, but the feathers in the mask gave away the peacock. Peter smiled. Miss Tree. *No, Caroline.* "If you'll excuse me, Eleanor."

Peter kept his eyes trained on her, walking through the ballroom as if there were no one else around. People stopped him to talk, but he offered an excuse and continued on his path. He stepped up behind Caroline and took hold of her hand. "Ah, you are a lovely peacock tonight." He pulled her forward, leading her away from the crowd. He had placed a kissing ball on the terrace outside. It was colder than he would have liked for spending time out of doors, but then again, if she were cold enough, would she let him hold her? When he had imagined this scene in his mind, she did.

He twisted the handle on the terrace doors, gently pushing Caroline out in front of him as he pulled the door closed behind him.

She stopped and looked up briefly, a smile forming on her lips when she saw the kissing ball. Peter stepped closer eliminating the distance between them. "I've been waiting for you all evening, Miss Tree." The terrace door opened, but he did not care who it was. No one would keep him from kissing Caroline tonight. He bent down and pressed a kiss to her lips as his hand reached back and pulled the string on her mask. He wanted to see Caroline as he kissed her, not Miss Tree.

The mask fell away at the same time a sharp intake of breath sounded behind him. Peter pulled back slightly and his eyes widening. Caroline was not the one behind the mask. It was Lady

Rockwell. She pulled him back down for another kiss. "I knew you still loved me, Peter."

He pulled back. "But I was certain..."

The terrace door slammed shut and Peter remembered the intake of breath. He pulled himself from Lady Rockwell's grip and moved to the door. A lady dressed in a similar blue-green iridescent gown rushed through the ballroom. Peter's hands shook as he reached for the knob.

He entered the ballroom just as the lady turned and looked back toward him, then fled from sight. It was Caroline.

Oh, lud. What have I done?

Peter started across the ball room after her, but he had only made it a handful of steps when Montjoy stepped in front of him. "What did you do to her? Did I not warn you against hurting her?" His chest rose and fell, anger rolling off of him.

Peter shook his head. "It is all a mistake. A misunderstanding. I need only talk to her." He tried to push past Montjoy, but he moved with him, blocking Peter's way.

"I believe you have said quite enough. Let her be."

A hand snaked its way around Peter's arm. He looked down into the smiling face of Lady Rockwell. "Peter, why did you rush off? You left me alone in the cold." Her lips turned down in a pout.

Peter pulled his arm from hers and stepped away. "That was a mistake, Lady Rockwell. I thought you someone else."

She scowled at him. "Yes, I am sure you did. But I am sure Lady Caroline will have nothing to do with you now. But I will still have you."

Peter stared at her. It sounded as if she had planned this, but how?

He looked toward the doorway Caroline had just left through and took a step toward it. Montjoy grabbed his arm. "I said to let her be."

Peter brushed Montjoy off and turned to Lady Rockwell. "Make my excuses. I find I am no longer in the mood for a masquerade ball."

He turned away from the crowd and walked back out the terrace doors, the cold wind a welcome distraction from the pain squeezing his chest.

❧ 19 ❧

Caroline stepped into the entryway looking wildly about. She did not wish to run into Peter or Samuel. Lady Kirtley and Lady Rockwell would not be a welcome sight either.

Lady Killingsworth stepped from the hallway Caroline had just left. "What do you think you are doing, Caroline, making such a scene?" She shook her head. "It is intolerable. Now turn around and return to the ball."

Caroline shook her head. "I cannot do that, my lady. I am feeling quite ill. I wish to return home."

"I will not allow it. You arrived beyond fashionably late and now you wish to leave early? It is not to be borne. Besides, if you do not return, you will be the subject of gossip. You are already much talked about, three and twenty and still not married." She grabbed Caroline by the arm and pulled her back toward the ballroom.

Caroline wrenched her arm from her mother's grasp. "No,

mother. I will not return. Can you not see I am upset? Do you not care for me at all?"

"Of course, I care for you. Do not be a dolt, child. But now is not the time to speak of it."

Caroline's head shook. "I am not returning." She took several steps back.

"I will not allow the carriage to be summoned. I do not know how you plan to return, but it shall not be with my help."

A small laugh escaped Caroline's mouth. "I have never asked for your help and you have never given it freely. Do not concern yourself, my lady. I shall find my own way home." She turned and walked away from the countess.

Caroline retrieved her wrap from the butler. "Shall I send for your carriage, my lady?"

Caroline shook her head. "No. I shall not be needing it." She stepped out into the cold night air and shivered. Her wrap was no match for the wind mingled with snow. She sat down on the top stair and dropped her head into her hands. What was she to do? It was only a mile to Whitley Wood if she took the back path, but in her thin dancing slippers and wrap she was sure to freeze before she reached the castle. Returning to the ball was not an option either, but sitting on the step seemed the most foolish option of all. At least if she was walking the exercise would help provide warmth. Caroline stood up and stepped down to the next step.

The door creaked open and Caroline spun around, ready to flee if Peter should appear.

Lady Kirtley poked her head out of the door. Her brow furrowed. "Lady Caroline? What are you doing out in this dreadful weather?"

Caroline wiped at her face, even though the wind had blown her tears dry long before they'd had a chance to fall. She gave a weak smile. "I was only thinking. I will be leaving shortly."

Lady Kirtley guffawed. "You will do no such thing. Come here, dear."

Caroline shook her head. "I would rather not return to the ball, my lady."

The door opened wider and Lady Kirtley waved her in. "I am not intending to take you back to the party. I thought a nice, quiet room by the fire would be more appropriate."

Caroline shivered uncontrollably. She could not stay out much longer or she would catch her death of a cold.

She nodded and turned to go back up the stairs. Stepping through the doorway, she allowed Lady Kirtley to lead her down a darkened corridor. At the end, she pushed open a door. The room was lit only by the glow from the coal burning low in the grate.

Lady Kirtley took a candle from the nearby stand and walked over to the fire to light it. She then proceeded to light several more candles, until the room was bathed in a warm glow.

She stepped to the bell chord and pulled, then settled onto the couch by the fire. "Would you join me? A maid should be here shortly to stoke the fire."

Caroline's teeth knocked together. No matter how hard she rubbed at her arms, she could not seem to infuse warmth into them.

Lady Kirtley held up a rug. "You look half frozen. Please, come sit down, Caroline."

Moving slowly, Caroline looked around the room. She had little reason to think Lady Kirtley was tricking her, but she also had little reason to think she would help her. They knew very little of each other. What cause would the older lady have to help her? The rug proved too enticing and Caroline hurried over and plucked it from the lady's hands. "Thank you, my lady."

Lady Kirtley tsked. "Please, call me Eleanor." Caroline sat

down and wrapped the blanket around her. It was warm from sitting close to the fire and she pulled it tighter around her.

A maid came in and stoked the fire. Caroline scooted down the settee, positioning herself as close to the fire as she could without sitting on the floor. Eleanor stood and spoke with the maid. The girl nodded.

"I thought tea might help you warm up. I sent Katie to fetch the water. And my tea chest."

Caroline squinted at her. "Should not Lady Rockwell hold the key to the chest? She is the mistress of the house, is she not?"

Lady Kirtley shrugged. "I was once the mistress of this house, after my mother died. It was only brief, but I find I have not given up the title easily. To eliminate the tensions, I brought my own with me."

Caroline nodded. What must Lady Kirtley think of Lady Rockwell—a woman younger than herself and her stepmother? She had said there were tensions, but Caroline had seen nothing to indicate the women did not get on well. And apart from the look of disappointment when Lady Rockwell sat next to Lady Kirtley on the hunt, they had been perfectly cordial to each other.

Caroline stood and moved in front of the fire, closing her eyes as the warmth finally seeped into her skin. "I would never have guessed there was tension between you and Lady Rockwell. When I have seen the two of you together, you have appeared quite amiable."

"We have learned to get along, in most cases, over the years. But there are still things we do not see in the same light."

Caroline wrapped the rug tighter around her, locking the warmth underneath as she sat back down next to Lady Kirtley. "And the tea is one of those things?"

Lady Kirtley chuckled. "Yes, I suppose it is."

She looked at the bottom of Caroline's dress, peeking out just below the rug wrapped around her. Lady Kirtley's eyes traveled to the mask hanging by its strings. "Peter was right." Her voice was quiet, but confident.

Caroline stiffened. She figured it was only a matter of time before his name was mentioned. The sound of his name both thrilled and angered her. She did not want to ask what he was right about, but her curiosity would not allow her to ignore the remark. "Excuse me?"

Eleanor moved to the edge of the couch, looking as though she were ready to pounce at any moment. "He told me of a young woman dressed as a peacock, whom he danced with in London. A woman named Miss Tree."

Caroline's face heated. Looking back on the incident, she could not account for what had provoked her to play such a game. It had seemed a harmless joke to keep her name from him, but now it only caused the hole she felt in her chest to enlarge.

"He was intrigued and most curious to discover the true identity of the woman." Lady Kirtley sighed. "He was convinced he had figured it out. Indeed, he hoped Miss Tree would come to this ball and it would confirm his suspicions."

Caroline swallowed but she could not bring herself to look up. "And did she come?"

A hand rested on Caroline's knee. "Why don't you tell me?"

"Why do you believe I should know?"

Lady Kirtley sat back. "Because Peter was convinced it was you. He *hoped* it was you."

Caroline let go of the rug, allowing it to drop down around her hips. She lifted the mask, running the peacock feathers though her fingers. He hoped it was her? What did that mean? She could not allow herself to believe the words at face value. Every time she believed...hoped her notions correct, she only ended up disappointed. What did it matter? He had chosen

Lady Rockwell. She waved the feathers back and forth in front of her.

"Caroline, are you Miss Tree?" Lady Kirtley tilted her head to one side, her gaze holding Caroline's.

She waved the peacock feathers around again. "I should think it obvious, is it not, my lady?"

"Eleanor," she said, correcting Caroline. "Peter thought that exact thing. Until the peacock he thought was you, turned out to be someone else entirely."

Caroline's brow furrowed. "What do you mean there was another peacock? Did he not remember my dress from London?"

"He is a man and not an observant one at that. There were only a few differences in the two dresses, but they were not overly obvious, especially to someone with no eye for fashion." She smiled at the slight against her own brother.

Caroline sat still for a moment. How would someone—not just someone, but Lady Rockwell—manage to have a gown so similar to Caroline's unless she had seen it in London. "But how did she even know about Miss Tree and the peacock costume?"

Eleanor took a deep breath. "I can only assume she overheard the conversation between Peter and me or saw you with him at Lord Trenton's ball. She will not confess her part. She realizes her mistake with Peter and believes there is a chance he will take her back."

Caroline dropped her gaze.

"She is wrong, you know," Eleanor said. "She will not get Peter back."

"How do you know?" Caroline's voice was barely a whisper.

"Because I believe him in love with someone else." Eleanor looked to the door and frowned. "What could be taking the tea so long? Perhaps she cannot locate my tea chest." Eleanor stood. "I shall go and investigate." She patted Caroline several times on the hand and smiled. "Please do not leave. I will return shortly."

Caroline watched Eleanor leave. She sat back into the corner of the settee, dropping the mask into her lap. She leaned her head back and closed her eyes, not certain what she felt or believed anymore. If what Eleanor said was true, Peter may possibly love her? Could he really have thought Lady Rockwell was her? The notion seemed unbelievable. Was it possible he was so focused on the costume that he did not take other factors into consideration?

She sighed. Lud, she hoped so.

The door opened, but Caroline kept her head back and her eyes closed. It felt so good to look at only blackness. It reminded her of the morning they had been sledding.

She heard the tea tray clatter lightly on the table. "It sounds as though you were able to find the maid."

"Yes, she was most obliging in allowing me to take it from her."

Caroline's eyes shot open at the sound of Peter's voice. "What are you doing here? Where is Lady Kirtley?"

He smiled at her, but his eyes held concern. "Eleanor was called away. She asked me to deliver the tea. She is quite worried you will catch a cold." He placed the tray on the table and cautiously sat on the settee. Reaching out, he ran his knuckles lightly over her cheeks. "You still feel chilled."

The heat she felt radiating from her face made her doubt his statement.

He glanced at the mask in her lap. "Where were you? I looked for you for more than an hour. And then when I spotted Miss Tree across the room, I..." He trailed off. "Tarnation, I have made a muddle of things." He leaned forward. Placing his elbows on his knees, he dropped his head into his hands and raked his fingers through his hair several times.

She wanted to touch him, but her hands shook. She clenched them tightly into fists and bit her lower lip. Miss Tree would have no qualms about reaching out to him. But she was not Miss Tree—not really. Miss Tree was a figment, a charade that need only be maintained for a set.

Could Caroline have more of Miss Tree in her than she realized? Her hand still trembled, but she ignored it as she placed it on his shoulder. "Perhaps not a complete muddle."

He lifted his head up and turned to look at her. "I was certain that peacock was you. I had planned everything out just so. I never considered that it could be someone else."

Caroline wanted to ask, but it felt so untoward. She took a deep breath and plunged ahead. "What was your plan? Will you tell me?"

He turned his body toward her. She could see hope in his eyes. He looked around the room. "There is no kissing ball in here."

Caroline licked her lips. "Let us pretend it is over there." She placed her mask over her face and tied the strings. Standing up, she walked to the far side of the room. "Pretend you are just seeing me for the first time tonight." She turned her back to him and stared at the wall. Would he play along? What if Eleanor was wrong and he did wish to be with Lady Rockwell?

A rustling at the settee sent gooseflesh up her arms and her pulse racing in her neck. She felt the heat from his body before he reached out to touch her.

His breath fluttered her hair and heat flooded her body, almost making her wish she were back outside. But only if Peter were with her.

"I have a surprise for you. Please, come with me." He reached for her hand and turned her around to face him. "This is where I made the mistake the last time."

Caroline put her finger to his lips. "We do not need to speak of your mistake."

His eyes flitted closed briefly. "I love your voice. Have I ever told you that?" He opened his eyes and stared at her. "It makes me feel like I'm floating in the pond with sunlight warming my body."

Caroline shivered. How was it possible to shiver as he spoke of warm sunlight?

He pulled her toward the imaginary kissing ball, dropping her hand when they were directly beneath it.

She frowned until he placed his hands on her hips.

He pulled her close to him, his arms tightening around her as he smiled down at her. "This is where my plan is a bit hazy. I practiced what to say, but it never felt right." He leaned down, his lips a breath away from hers. "If Montjoy or Eleanor or anyone else interrupts us this time, I will not be responsible for what happens next."

Caroline grinned back at him. "Then I suggest you quit soliloquizing and move on with your plan."

He closed the distance and she let her eyes flutter shut. His lips brushed hers before covering them fully with his own. Color popped in the darkness behind her eyelids as Peter intensified the kiss.

Perhaps it was better they had not kissed under the kissing ball on Christmas Eve. Caroline was certain she would have made a complete cake of herself, wanting more of his kisses.

He pulled back, and her eyes drifted open. Was that all? She wanted more. She rose up on her tip toes, bringing her arms around his neck.

He pulled her tighter to him, chuckling softly in her ear before he kissed her on the earlobe.

She could no longer tell his heartbeat from hers.

He reached up her back, tugging at the string holding her mask to her face. It fell away and he bent back down, brushing a kiss along her cheek. "I want to see the whole of your face when I kiss you," he whispered against her flushed skin.

"Why?" She needed to know this was not just what men did, that he felt for her what she felt for him.

"Why? Do you really not know?" He placed his hand on her check.

She leaned into his hand. "I know what I wish you to say, but I should like to hear it in your voice."

"I love you, Caroline." His voice was low and husky. He bent his head lower, kissing her shoulder and moving up her neck.

She was grateful he held her tightly, unsure her legs would hold her. "Why do you love me?"

He stared down at her. "What is there not to love? You are kind, witty and immensely clever, Miss Tree. You make me feel things I have never felt before."

She arched a brow at him.

"For years, almost since my mother died, I have been restless. No place could hold my attention for long. But since being here with you, I have not felt that need to find something better. There is no restlessness." He ran his knuckles down her cheek. "It has been a part of me for as long as I can remember, but now it is gone. This is the best it could ever be. If you are with me, I am complete."

She rested her head against his chest, his heart pounded against her ear. "But will you always feel this way?"

He pulled back and lifted her chin with his finger. "Always."

She smiled and pulled away. "There is something I need to fetch. Please, stay here?"

He nodded but did not release her hand. "I do not want to ever let you go."

She came willingly when he tugged her back to him. "Why can I not go with you?"

She raised a brow. "If you wish to take the risk of being pulled back into the party..."

He pressed a kiss to her lips, cutting off her words. "Very well, I shall let you go alone. But I suggest you make haste. I will not wait patiently for long."

She brushed her hand down the side of his face. "Still my impatient, Peter."

She slipped from the room and down the corridor to the alcove just to the side of the ballroom door, grateful she had chosen this side, rather than the other. Had she placed her package in the alcove on the other side, she risked being seen by those inside the ballroom.

Snatching the brown paper parcel, she turned and fled back down the darkened corridor.

The door pushed silently open and she slipped inside. Peter paced in front of the fireplace; his hands clasped behind his back.

He stopped and turned toward her when she closed the door.

She moved to the settee and sat down, patting the seat next to her.

He sat down close, his thigh settling next to hers.

She placed the package in his lap. "I know I should wait until tomorrow to give this to you, but I doubt we will have much privacy then."

He picked it up and turned it over in his hands, his brow furrowed.

Lifting a hand, she gently ran her fingers over his brow. His face relaxed under her touch. How had she waited so long to do it?

He worked the twine to one end and slipped it off the package. The paper fell open revealing the book of maps they had looked at in the village.

He looked up at her. "I went back for it, but it was gone."

She ran her tongue over her bottom lip. "Perhaps if you begin to feel restless, we can look at this and plan a trip together."

He placed the book on the floor against the settee. "I shall never go anywhere without you." He intertwined her fingers with his. "Tell me, do you think your uncle will be able to find another chaperone for your cousin? I think you will be unable to provide him that service any longer."

EPILOGUE

Caroline wiggled the ring on her fourth finger with her thumb, her gloves prohibiting it from moving very far.

She looked up at the town house and sighed. This ball felt different than any other she had attended. Perhaps it was because for the first time, she was attending as a married woman.

Fingers threaded through hers and Peter pulled her in close to his side. He smiled down at her and pressed a kiss to her temple. "You are sure to be the most tempting armful in attendance tonight."

His words delighted her. Now that they were married, he did not have to say such things. She knew of many couples who never shared such intimacies once the vows had been spoken.

But Peter was different. She had yet to be in his company when he did not offer some sort of compliment or words of affection. He made her feel loved and wanted—something she had not felt in years.

She felt his hand at the small of her back, and a tingle ran up her spine.

He bent down. "Your thin wrap is no match for the cold. Let us get inside where it is warm." His breath on her neck made her skin erupt in gooseflesh.

They made their way up the steps and into Mr. Barrington's house. They had barely handed off their coats and wraps to the footman when Prudence appeared at Caroline's side.

"I do not understand why you could not continue as my chaperone, just because you are now married." She scowled and cast a dark look over her shoulder. "The dragon will not allow me to leave her sight."

Caroline could not help but grin. She shifted, leaning back slightly on her heels, her hands clasped lightly in front of her. "Did you not tell my uncle you did not wish me to return to London with you? I have only done as you requested." The sweetness in Caroline's voice did nothing to erase the sulk from Prudence's face.

She narrowed her eyes at Caroline and Peter. "I blame you for this, Lord Rockwell."

He grinned. "I am content to take full responsibility." He pulled Caroline closer to him. "Perhaps next time you are allowed the company of one as sweet as your dear cousin, you will take a kinder approach."

Prudence stomped her foot. "She was not so very kind to me." She narrowed her gaze at Caroline. "I have not forgotten your part with Mr. Thurston. But you were far more amiable than Miss Brown. Even her name is dull and boring."

The dull and boring woman sidled up next to Prudence. She dipped a slight curtsy to Caroline and Peter. "My Lord and Lady Rockwell."

Caroline smiled. "Miss Brown. How good it is to see you this evening. Your gown is quite lovely. The color suits you very well."

The older woman colored up, obviously not accustomed to compliments.

Prudence eyed her companion up and down. "That drab old thing? It does nothing for her complexion. Why—" Her gaze caught on something and she waved off the conversation, drifting toward the ballroom instead.

Miss Brown dipped another quick curtsy, her gaze never leaving Prudence. "It was pleasant to see you again, my lady." She hurried into the crowded ballroom.

Caroline sighed. "Oh, I do not envy the woman. She has a mighty task ahead of her."

Peter placed his hand around her waist and guided her to the receiving line. "Come, let us greet our hosts and then we can move inside and watch poor Miss Brown and Miss Winslow. I believe this performance may just turn out to be a comedy."

Caroline swatted at his arm with her fan, but a grin twitched at her lips. "Be kind. I am sure Prudence will do all in her power to cause Miss Brown consternation. It is what Prudence does best." Caroline motioned to the ballroom. "I see Mr. Benton is here tonight. It will be a long evening for Miss Brown."

Peter hurried her along. "All the more reason for us to get inside and find the best seats for watching."

Caroline leaned her head against his shoulder as they waited for their turn in line. "Thank you, Peter."

He looked down. "For what are you thanking me?"

She signed contentedly. "For everything; for ending my time as a companion, for bringing me to London. But foremost, for loving me."

He dropped a kiss on her head. "You are easy to love, my dear." He looked around exaggeratedly. "On second thought, I am not so much in the mood for a comedy. What do you say we return to Rockwell House and enjoy a quiet evening at home?" He raised his brows in quick succession several times.

The love in his eyes nearly took Caroline's breath away. "We have already been seen by Mr. Barrington. If we should cry off now, without a proper greeting, I am afraid it will not end well." She placed a finger to her lips and Peter growled low in his throat.

Caroline laughed. "But once we have seen our hosts, I see no reason to stay on a moment longer."

He brought her fingers to his lips, his eyes sparkling with mischief. "Oh, Lady Rockwell. I do love you."

PREVIEW OF GOODWILL FOR THE GENTLEMAN

December 19, 1813-London, England

Lieutenant Hugh Warrilow put an anxious hand to the strings holding up his eagle mask. The mask was large enough to conceal his face, but the strings seemed flimsy, not nearly secure enough to ensure his anonymity.

The mask was the one thing which had persuaded him to venture out in public, and he was already regretting his decision.

He looked at the hordes of people in the ballroom of Lord Trenton's London townhouse: hooded, masked, and glittering. There was a sense of safety in numbers—it was comforting to be lost amidst a crowd. Besides, no one knew he was back in England. No one would expect to see him there—or even expect him to be alive, perhaps.

But he couldn't help feeling that it was reckless to attend such an event. What if his mask were to somehow come undone? He had no desire to face the whispers and rumors.

"I thought you said it was a private gathering," he said to Captain Gillingham, a touch of annoyance in his voice.

"And so it is," Gillingham responded cheerfully through his turtle mask, admiring the woman passing by in a shimmering gown meant to resemble fish scales. "Hardly a soul here! Everyone's left town already for the holidays."

Hugh scoffed. "You could have fooled me. It bears a strong resemblance to the last masquerade I attended at Vauxhall Gardens three years ago—and that was hardly exclusive."

"Bah! Vauxhall would have ten times this many people. I'll tell you what—you've become too accustomed to solitude." Gillingham clapped Hugh on the back of his black domino. "Come, Warrilow."

Hugh grabbed his friend's arm. "Don't use my name, for heaven's sake," he said through a tight jaw, glancing around to see if anyone was listening.

Gillingham shot him a troubled look. "If you're heading for home, Warrilow, it's only a matter of time before it's out that you've returned."

"Yes," said Hugh, "but I would much rather that the news come out when I am *not* here to witness its effect."

Gillingham clucked his tongue. "This won't do at all! Let down your hair. Live a little. It's high time you enjoyed yourself for a change. One doesn't take a leave of absence to go hide in a cave, man!"

"If one has my reputation, one just might," Hugh said dryly.

It was foolish to have let Gilllingham persuade him into coming. The only thing standing between him and appalled glances was his mask. He *should* have made his way home from Spain directly to the family estate at Norfield—as he had planned to do—rather than agreeing to break his journey in London for a few days. Or he might have even gone to Grindleham, the Warrilows' small estate in Derbyshire, for a chance to adjust to life in England before seeing him family. And yet, here he was.

Gillingham had always had a way of cajoling Hugh into agreeing to his plans.

"Your reputation?" Gillingham spat out. "That was years ago. You know as well as I that society has a memory for scandal shorter than Prinny's breath."

Hugh wished he could believe that. He wished his *own* memory was as fickle as Gillingham seemed to think the *ton's* memory was. But surely one never forgot the looks and whispers which had followed Hugh so doggedly, until he had decided to accept his uncle's offer to buy a commission. In many ways, the battlefield had been a welcome reprieve.

He rubbed at his shoulder and winced. Of course, not all of it had been a reprieve. Not by any stretch of the imagination.

Gillingham shook his head, his eyes wide with wonder behind his black domino as he admired the scene. "I had forgotten how much I missed England. No offense to *las señoritas españolas*, of course," he added quickly, "but I am tolerably certain that nothing can compare to an accomplished English lady."

Hugh was silent, but he found himself in agreement with his friend. He had been close enough to swearing off his home country forever, to staying in Spain where he had a fresh start, a clean slate. But there was something extraordinary about England and her people.

Hugh was glad to be back.

Of course, for all his family knew, he was still in Spain. Just as likely, they thought him dead.

It had been months and months since he had written to them, after all.

He worried his lip, thinking about the reception he was likely to receive from them. Whatever their reactions might be, he could hardly blame them after he had neglected to inform them of his injury and his intent to return.

He had his reasons, though. At first, the ball in his shoulder had prevented it. Then it was the subsequent illness and the all-encompassing grief at losing Robert Seymour.

He shook his head. He didn't want to think on that right now. There would be more than enough time for it once he was back at Norfield.

Regardless, holding a quill to paper had been the last thing on his mind after his injury. And then it had been easy to continue putting it off for one reason or another. Before he knew it, he had begun to wonder if perhaps his family wasn't better off without him—better off believing him dead or disappeared like the coward so many believed him to be.

But in the end, he realized he couldn't stay away from England, from his mother—from his past. Everyone else might come to forget him in his absence, forget the shame he bore, but he wouldn't have forgotten, no matter how long he stayed away.

Gillingham grabbed his arm with an intake of breath. "Come. I must dance with that young woman over there." He indicated a young lady wearing a gold domino and cat ears, standing—quite strangely—alone.

"Do you know her?"

"No," Gillingham reasoned, "but how is *she* to know that? After all, a masquerade is the only ball where I can conceivably approach a stranger and ask her to dance." He grinned, and Hugh shook his head with a chuckle, following alongside him.

He would accompany Gillingham without complaint, but it was a waste of time for Hugh to set his own sights on any of the women in attendance. At least he assumed so. Who would wish to dance with a man reputed to be a jilt? Of course, his mask kept them from *knowing* such a thing, but it felt wrong to take advantage of their ignorance.

"My lady," Gillingham said in his most alluring voice as they came upon the young woman.

She turned, and Hugh noted her almond-shaped eyes of blue-flecked gray, which peered at him through her cat mask. He felt his heart rate pick up slightly and shook away the thought of two women he knew with just such pairs of eyes.

"Might I persuade you," Gillingham continued, "to stand up with me for the next set?" He extended a hand toward her, dipping into an overly-formal bow.

A woman in a tiger mask and an orange- and black-striped, hooded domino approached them, coming shoulder-to-shoulder with the woman in the cat mask as she glanced at Gillingham's extended hand.

"Lucy," she said, shooting a watchful glance at Hugh and Gillingham. "I thought you were with Mr. Pritchard or I shouldn't have left you."

Hugh stilled, glancing back and forth between the two women, his wide eyes lingering on the hooded one: her confident posture, her direct gaze, the color of her caramel brown hair that peeked out from her hood. He would recognize her anywhere, domino or no.

It was Emma Caldwell, the woman he had loved—the woman he hoped fervently that he didn't *still* love—and beside her Lucy Caldwell, the woman he had jilted.

Hugh's jaw clenched, and he suppressed the impulse to check that his mask was still on. He wasn't ready to face the Caldwells. Not just yet.

His first act upon arrival in England had been to inquire as subtly as possible whether the Caldwell sisters were—as he assumed they would be—married. He had hoped that Emma, at least, would have married, for it would have been a type of forced closure to his abominably persistent affection.

But neither had married during his absence. This was perhaps not a surprise for Emma, as she had often proclaimed her lack of desire to marry. But Lucy...he trusted that she had reasons beyond any related to Hugh and his purposeful rejection of her.

Either way, he had to do what he came to do: repair the brokenness he'd left behind him when he'd gone off to war. He had to face up to it, and that meant making things right with Lucy—it meant offering now what he hadn't been able to bring himself to offer three years ago: marriage.

At the time, he had rationalized his choice—they hadn't been formally engaged, after all. But the arrangement between the families had been of longstanding: that Hugh, the heir of Norfield would marry Lucy, the eldest of the Caldwells. It had made perfect sense to his own parents and to Lucy's parents.

But it had made no sense to Hugh's heart, which had stubbornly latched onto Emma and dug in its heels at any of Hugh's attempts to change its affections. His heart simply refused to give up the confident, bold protector he had seen Emma become. How ironic that it was what he loved so well about Emma that had ensured she would never forgive him.

But, hated by Emma or no, he had simply not been able to subject Lucy to marrying a man who was in love with her sister.

He'd had three years away from Emma, though—long enough, he hoped, for his heart to see sense; or at least to subject itself to his strengthened determination. He knew now that there were more important things in life than following his heart: he had a duty to his family and to Norfield. Lucy might reject his offer of marriage, and she might well hate him, but Hugh was prepared to face that if it meant a chance of righting the wrong he had done years ago—a chance to prove himself.

At least Lucy would no longer be laboring under the misapprehension that he was some sort of *nonpareil,* as she had thought him to be before it had all happened.

A man strode up, his fiery red hair set off by the green of his domino, his face masked in black. He bowed slightly to Hugh and Gillingham before offering an arm to the young woman in gold—to Lucy.

"Ah, my apologies," Gillingham said, clearing his throat. "I see that I am too late in my request." He smiled at the man in the blue domino without any rancor. "But don't let that prevent the two of you—" he indicated Hugh and Emma — "from joining the set."

Hugh clenched his teeth, wanting nothing more than to strangle his friend. But that was not an option, and for the first time in three years, Emma's eyes looked at him.

He had been haunted by those gray eyes since his sudden departure; haunted by the cold contempt they had held when she had last looked on him. Any flicker of hope he had been harboring that she would forgive him for jilting Lucy had disappeared in that moment.

His first inclination was to make his excuses to Emma, to avoid the prospect of standing up together for a set. If they danced, she was bound to discover his identity, and what would she do then? She was quite capable of deserting him on the dance floor. He could almost see the look of revulsion that would transform her otherwise-kind eyes.

He shuddered slightly. The prospect was too reminiscent of their last encounter. It brought flashbacks of the humiliation that had consumed him and the astounded faces that had surrounded him when she had given him the cut direct in just such a ballroom as this.

A fourth gentleman joined the group, coming up beside Emma. Hugh swallowed the lump in his throat. Who was the gentleman? According to a mutual acquaintance, she wasn't married. But was she engaged? His heart dropped.

"I am afraid I must ask your pardon," Emma said. "I am promised to stand up with Mr. Douglas." She indicated the man beside her.

Hugh bowed politely, feeling relief as well as regret, then put a firm hand on Gillingham's shoulders and pulled him away.

"Confound it," Gillingham said. "Should have known the angel would be spoken for with a smile like that. I should have asked her to save me the next set, but with that fellow's eyes boring into me, I lost my nerve."

Hugh was silent, feeling the beads of sweat which were gathering at his hairline. How had he not considered that he might happen upon the Misses Caldwell at the masquerade? He had assumed that they would already be at home for Christmas. The Caldwells took the holiday season very seriously.

It hadn't taken him more than two minutes in Emma's presence, though, to feel the magnetic draw to her; the pull that he fervently hoped had dissipated during his time on the Continent.

But perhaps it was simply the unexpectedness of the encounter in combination with his nerves that he had mistaken for lingering romantic attraction?

He sincerely hoped so.

***

The violins strung out the last notes of a cotillion, and Emma's partner, Mr. Douglas, bowed. She took the opportunity to steal a curious glance at the man her sister Lucy was promised to marry, who was making his bow next to Mr. Douglas.

Mr. George Pritchard was nothing like the sort of man she had expected Lucy to wed, with his close-cropped red hair, freckles, and bland gaze.

He must have felt Emma's eyes on him, since he looked over at her as he straightened. He offered an abashed smile before turning his head away, as if embarrassed he had caught her looking at him.

She kept her eyes on him, one side of her mouth tilting upward at his behavior. At least he was kind. Perhaps that was all that mattered.

"It was an honor to stand up with you, Miss Caldwell," said Mr. Douglas, taking a step toward her.

She smiled politely. A dance with Mr. Douglas was very much like any other dance—full of civil small-talk and polite smiles. But that was what Emma needed: someone ordinary and reliable; someone she could respect but never fall in love with; someone with the ability to make her comfortable but without the ability to hurt her.

"I understand," Mr. Douglas continued, "that you are to journey home for the holidays."

She nodded. "Yes, my mother is staunchly traditional, you know, and she insists that we all return home to celebrate the season together. It is her idea of heaven, and she guards it somewhat aggressively."

Mr. Douglas nodded his understanding. "She is German, is she not?"

"Yes, and very proud of it, too," Emma said with a significant look. "At this time of year more than any other."

"I should very much like to meet her. Allow me to wish you a very happy Christmas with your family. I hope that, once your father has returned to town, I might perhaps beg an audience with him." His brows raised in a question.

Emma felt her stomach clench oddly. Ignoring a silly reaction to a very expected comment, she nodded with a smile and bid him goodbye.

It was precisely what she had been planning for, so there was no reason to regard a bit of unease. Surely it was natural to feel nervous at the prospect of marriage, something she had been putting off for so long.

She turned to Lucy, who was watching Mr. Pritchard walk off, his blue domino sweeping behind him.

"He is very amiable, Lucy. I think you have done well." Emma tilted her head as she watched him. "Though he is perhaps not precisely the type of gentleman I had pictured you marrying."

Lucy turned toward her, drawing her head back slightly with a frown. "What kind of gentleman *did* you think I should marry?" Her voice was soft, just like her kind eyes and the ringlets which hung loosely on her shoulders.

Emma narrowed her eyes in thought. "I think I assumed that you would marry someone a bit taller. More imposing and protective. And though I am beginning to think it very distinguished, the red hair was certainly unexpected." She sent Lucy a teasing smile.

"Oh?" Lucy said, amused. "I had no idea you had such an opinion on the matter. Anything else, pray?"

Emma nodded with a teasing smile. It was absurd of her to have acquired such strong beliefs about the appearance and character of Lucy's future husband. And yet she *had* acquired them. "Perhaps just one or two more things: formidable on first inspection, but with a soft light in his eyes and a kind heart."

Emma was only half teasing. Lucy needed someone to guard the quiet, sensitive woman she was—to protect her from any more pain. She needed a gentle gentleman. Mr. Pritchard was both gentle and a gentleman, of course. He simply looked too slight to act as much of a protector.

"This is all very enlightening. And what if *I* should take it upon myself to find a husband for you?" Lucy suggested.

Emma let out a small laugh, and she wrapped her arm into Lucy's. "I think you would do a fine job of choosing a husband for me—if only I hadn't already decided upon one myself."

Lucy ignored her words, scanning the crowd until her eyes stopped. "Hmm...what of Lord Whitfield?"

Emma followed her sister's gaze to the earl. He wore no costume, providing quite a contrast to his friend beside him, dressed in a very extravagant lion costume.

Emma looked at Lucy with incredulous brows. "Perhaps we shouldn't aim quite so high, Lucy."

Lucy sighed. "Very well." She continued scanning the room. "Ah, and what about the man in the black, eagle mask from earlier? The one you were to dance with? There was something a bit mysterious about him, I think, and *everyone* likes mystery."

Emma laughed. "Mysterious? Perhaps because he didn't say a single word? *Or* because he is wearing an enormous bird mask. The entire purpose of a masquerade is to give us the illusion of mystery, isn't it?"

"There would be less mystery if you danced with him." Lucy wagged her brows once. "Or married him, even," she said with a playful shrug.

Emma clucked her tongue. "As I said, it is a terrible shame that I have already settled upon who I am to marry."

Lucy sighed, giving up the game. "Mr. Douglas?"

Emma nodded with a laugh. "Why should you say it in such a voice? He is perfectly respectable."

"Never mind," Lucy said resignedly. "Are you sure you don't wish to travel with us to Barthorpe Hall? We leave tomorrow morning, and George insists it would be no trouble at all to have you stay there with us for two or three days. We will be to Marsdon by the 23rd at the very latest, in plenty of time to help Mama decorate."

Emma smiled but shook her head. "It is very kind of him, but I still have a number of things to do before leaving town." She shifted her jaw, thinking of the letter she had received. "Besides,

I've just received a letter from Papa. He has asked that I break my journey for dinner at Norfield to convey his congratulations and a gift to Alfred and his new fiancée." She shot Lucy a significant look. "I doubt that is something you would like to do—particularly in the company of George." If George Pritchard knew of Lucy's past with Hugh Warrilow, it would likely be uncomfortable for him.

Lucy's own eyebrows shot up. "Surely between you and me, there is little doubt who relishes the thought of a visit to Norfield Manor less. You can't even bring yourself to *say* Hugh Warrilow's name—how will you fare, dining at his home where he is very likely to come up in conversation? Where there will be reminders of him everywhere?"

Emma said nothing for a moment. His was a name that made her blood boil, even three years later.

Lucy sought her eyes. "You prove my point with your silence." She sighed and shook her head. "How you can go from cheering on a match between Hugh and myself, touting his best qualities, to despising him so—it isn't reasonable, Emma."

Emma *had* thought Hugh a wonderful match for Lucy at one time. In fact, Emma's description—*imposing but kind and gentle*—was an apt description of the man Emma had once thought Hugh was—the perfect man to protect Lucy's pure and guileless heart.

But instead of shielding Lucy as he should have, he had left her vulnerable, subjected her to scorn and heartache.

Emma clenched one of her gloved hands. The memory of Lucy's anguish—her lovely, kind eyes set within two dark hollows, the way they filled up with tears at the least provocation—it still felt fresh to Emma. Lucy would be a married woman soon and seemed to have moved past what had happened, but Emma could never forget how Lucy's broken heart had seemed to break her spirit for so long.

Emma took a glass of negus from the silver tray held by a passing footman and handed it to Lucy before taking one for herself. "I am very fond of Lady Dayton, and I have no need to fret over being confronted by Hugh Warrilow—"

"I believe he is a lieutenant now," Lucy said.

Emma tilted her head. "I am sure you are right. But who is to say, when he has made no effort to write his family? He could be anywhere, in any state, really." She shrugged lightly. "I think it likely that he has met the same sad fate as so many other soldiers have."

Lucy lowered her glass. "If that is so, it is not something to take pleasure in, Emma. It is terribly sad. Lady Dayton only recently told me that she feels she must accept that he is dead. And I fear she may be right. Mrs. Seymour's husband was fighting in Spain, too, you know, and *she* received the tragic news of his death months ago. That Lord and Lady Dayton have had not a word from Hugh for so long does not bode well."

Emma pursed her lips. "How can you be so charitable to one who hurt you so? I suppose I should be cast down at the thought of him killed in battle, and indeed I am very sorry for Lady Dayton's sake. But I shall never be able to forgive Hugh—*Lieutenant Warrilow*"— she said on seeing Lucy open her mouth to speak —"for how he hurt my dearest sister." She reached a hand to Lucy's face, brushing her gloved thumb over her cheek.

Lucy's cheeks were rosy again now, even without rouge. They hadn't always been, though. For so long after Hugh Warrilow's departure, her face had been pale, wan, and thinner than usual.

Lucy frowned. "You are much too critical of him, Emma."

She always looked grave when Emma spoke her mind about Hugh Warrilow.

"He is a good, kind man," Lucy said, "much better than you give him credit for. And I harbor him no ill-will." She inclined her head. "To be sure, it is not a time of my life I should ever choose to repeat, but"— she put a hand up to silence Emma's retort —"I shouldn't wished to have married him, knowing he was so opposed to it."

"You were *engaged*, Lucy," Emma said, setting her empty glass down on the tray held by a passing footman.

"Not officially," Lucy said. "We never courted." She shook her head. "It was not official."

Emma shrugged her shoulders. "It may as well have been. Everyone knew that you were meant to wed."

Lucy paused before answering. "Yes. But that was no fault of his. Besides, he received punishment enough from friends and acquaintances afterward. Including you." She looked Emma in the eye with a hint of censure.

Lucy had not been at all thrilled upon discovering that Emma had given him the cut direct after everything had happened. No matter how devastated she had been to learn that her love was unrequited and that she was not to marry him after all, Lucy had been a staunch defender of Hugh Warrilow.

Emma would never understand it. Nor could she find it in herself to regret what she had done. She could hardly have stood up to dance with the man who had just shattered Lucy's heart and then dared to show up to a ball—all while Lucy was too devastated to get out of bed.

Emma would have done anything to take on Lucy's heartache in her stead.

"Well," Emma said, perking up, "I am sure that—if he *is* alive— he is kicking himself for having turned down the opportunity to marry a woman with a heart as kind and good as yours. That you have forgiven him says nothing at all about him but *everything* good about you, my sweet Lucy."

"Much as you pretend that it is not the case," Lucy said, "*you* have the more loyal and kind heart between the two of us, Emma."

"Bah," Emma said, holding her chin up with feigned hauteur, "my heart has nothing to say to anything."

"Perhaps," Lucy said hesitantly, "that is only because you have not yet found the gentleman it responds to."

"Then I hope I never shall. I shall marry for convenience or not at all, Lucy."

"And that is why you are accepting the attentions of Mr. Douglas?"

"Yes," Emma said baldly.

"But you have nothing at all in common," said Lucy, an almost pleading note to her voice.

"*That* is precisely why his suit is appealing. I shan't have to worry about one of us falling in love with the other. Both of us are reasonable, neither given to romantics; I think we shall suit well enough."

Emma's eyes sought out Mr. Douglas, who had removed his mask entirely and was standing beside his younger sister. He was a very practical man, as was demonstrated by the neat clothing visible underneath his equally-plain domino.

It was something Emma appreciated about him, as she glanced around the room at the vibrant waistcoats, intricate cravats, and high collars, many of which were beginning to wilt due to the warmth of the ball. Unless one stood near one of the windows where a frigid breeze blew in from outside, the humid heat generated by candles, fires, and dozens of bodies in the ballroom was stifling. Emma's hooded domino only added to the oppressive heat.

She was very much looking forward to a respite from the unending string of balls and parties they had been attending in anticipation of Parliament's holiday recess.

Lucy heaved a sigh. "Is it wrong of me to say, Emma, that I want more for you than Mr. Douglas?"

Emma saw Lucy's eyes on the man and suddenly felt defensive. It was unlike Lucy to say anything uncomplimentary. She could find it in her to defend the man who had jilted her, but she could find nothing good to say of Mr. Douglas?

"Wanted more for me?" Emma said. "What more? My own Mr. Pritchard? My own version of Hugh Warrilow to jilt me?"

Lucy was silent, and Emma glanced at her with a stab of guilt. She squeezed her eyes shut. "I am sorry, Lucy. That was terribly cruel. Please forgive me. I think that this heat has made me irritable. You know that I have never had a great interest in marrying." She smiled wryly. "I only entertain the notion now because I overheard Mrs. Richins claiming that I couldn't convince a shopkeeper to offer for me now that I am on the shelf. Naturally I must prove her wrong."

Lucy was in too grave a humor to laugh at Emma's jest, and Emma took her hand. "What do you say to this, Lucy? If Mr. Douglas doesn't come up to scratch and offer for me, I give you leave to choose my husband for me."

Lucy smiled weakly, looking Emma in the eye. "You were meant to love deeply, Emma. I just know it. It is why I am saddened at the prospect of you marrying without any affection at all."

Emma sighed. "Oh Lucy, I don't have a heart like yours. I think you would love any person you married. *Your* heart holds enough warmth to make up for the coldness of mine."

Lucy shook her head emphatically, her ringlets, swaying to and fro. "Your heart is anything but cold—I know that better than anyone. You may not give your heart easily, but once given, it is secure. It is what I love so much about you: I never need doubt you."

Emma squeezed Lucy's hand. "That last part, at least, is true."

It was too like Lucy to believe the best of everyone. It was what had allowed her to forgive Hugh Warrrilow so readily. But Lucy's tendency to think the best of every person she encountered was what had resulted in her heart being broken.

And though she might sometimes envy Lucy's optimism, Emma felt more secure, more able to protect Lucy from further pain by being the more practical and realistic of the two.

It was that pragmatism that led her to desire a marriage of convenience.

Lucy might not be satisfied with Emma marrying Mr. Douglas, but Emma was perfectly content with her decision. Or at least tolerably so.

Goodwill for the Gentleman by Martha Keyes

AFTERWORD

Dear Reader,

Thank you so much for reading! I hope you love this story as much as I do.

As is the case for most of my stories, the castles and estates houses are based on actual places. Whitley Wood Castle was based on Restormel Castle. While this castle is now in ruins, I can imagine what it looked like in its prime. I loved the idea of a circular castle, complete with a drawbridge and a mote. Wirksworth Hall was loosely based on Batsford House.

Be sure to check out my other stories:
    Mistaken Identity
    Reforming the Gambler
    Miss Marleigh's Pirate Lord
    An American in Duke's Clothing
    The Baron's Rose

Happy reading!
Mindy

ABOUT THE AUTHOR

Mindy loves all things history and romance, which makes reading and writing romance right up her alley. Since she was a little girl, playing in her closet "elevator," she has always had stories running through her mind. But it wasn't until she was well into adulthood, that she realized she could write those stories down. Now they occupy her dreams and most every quiet moment she has-she often washes her hair two or three times because she was thinking about her stories when she did it the first time. Which usually means really clean hair and a fixed plot hole. When she isn't living in her alternate realities, she is married to her real-life Mr. Darcy and trying to raise five proper boys. They live happily in the beautiful mountains of Utah.

Manufactured by Amazon.ca
Bolton, ON

20464170R00125